LEGACIES
of a
Mormon
Family:

A NOVEL

by

James Farmer
Cartwright

Legacies of a Mormon Family:
A Novel
by
James Farmer Cartwright

Cover image: Draper Ward and Roundhouse,
photograph in Draper Historical Society
collection. Used by permission, via email from
Ms. Esther Kinder, secretary, 22 Sept. 2021.

CONTENTS

iii

[This page left intentionally blank.]

ACKNOWLEDGEMENTS

I am grateful to the participants of Writers' Workshop at Lutheran Church of Honolulu and in particular to Dr. Kathryn Klingebiel, PhD, who chaired the workshop from its inception until January 2020. Over several years, I have read portions of this novel to them and received valuable suggestions and immense encouragement. Dr. Klingebiel suggested the inclusion of the "Mormon Vocabulary" at the end of the novel.

I thank several friends who have encouraged me through the years. Primary among these is my spouse, Wally Mahan.

Dr. Tia Ballantine, PhD, has contributed immensely to the quality of this novel. My rewriting following her comment that the whole novel needed serious reorganization has made the work much better. On a second reading, she made some stylistic changes. I employed some; others changes I rejected, retaining my original wording. This process helped me find my voice, for which I am grateful. Whatever stylistic errors exist are my responsibility.

Finally, Stan Baptista has helped immensely in technology of formatting the final version, including the cover creation. Without his guidance, I could not have this novel published.

INTRODUCTION

The characters in *Legacies* live and love within Mormon society. In Part I, CT Reynolds is a third generation Mormon whose grandparents anchored their lives through the Mormon exile, walking from Iowa to the Salt Lake Valley in Utah. CT lives in the milieu of the Church as it modified its policies to merge with American reality, no longer actively practicing polygamy, abandoning the theocratic political order, facing the challenges of scientific discovery vis a vis the religious beliefs of the mid nineteenth century, questioning authority in all aspects. Emma, the woman CT meets and marries, finds her challenges as well, not only in her relationship with CT, but in her struggles with self-worth versus societal expectations.

The second part of *Legacies* focuses on the family's struggles almost twenty years after Part I ends. As Caleb, the son of CT and Emma, begins college, he struggles with the same challenges of obedience to authority in contrast to the realities in his life experiences. During Caleb's college years, actions which seemed suggestive of homosexuality were disparaged. As he wrestles between his reality and Church teaching, he obeys. He serves a mission for the LDS Church. He dates women. He serves in callings in the Church. Following the counsel of his bishop, he marries Belle, the woman he has befriended, without revealing to her his attraction to men. Both suffer.

In addition to the challenge of her marriage to a gay man, Belle faces the challenges women in general face between conflicting ideas of obedience to authority and individual needs for freedom to search for knowledge, to learn, and to act.

As the various stories of *Legacies* unfold, it is perhaps logical that readers might vilify certain characters, but there are no villains here, only mortals who make mistakes. Often these mistakes cause others to suffer; those who err suffer as well. Frequently these mistakes stem from people accepting the dictates of "higher authorities" who almost always mean well but allow society to set norms not borne out by reality, facts, and truth.

These challenges are not unique to Mormon society, per se. In twentieth-century America, members of religious communities and ethnic groups emigrating from throughout the world have the challenge of deciding where each person stands in conflicts between authority and individual reality, between obedience and changing societal norms. The same conflicts emerge in the lives of many cultural and age groups today.

I wrote these stories as fiction. Most place names are real, though I have occasionally altered some names. This may suggest that the accounts herein are factual accounts of real people in the past. That is incorrect; while stories, characters, and incidents may spring from reality, they are fiction. Some of the incidents grow out of my personal story; the blessing CT gives his son Caleb, e.g., mirrors the blessing my father gave me immediately prior to my going to San Francisco in the spring of 1961. Many years later that blessing became vital to me as I made my journey of coming out as a gay man. Hence the dedication of Part II, Promises, to Papa, my father.

From the 1950s to the present time, official pronouncements from Mormon Church authorities have repeatedly scorned homosexual behavior. Some influential Church authorities have denied the existence of homosexuals, insisting that men are all heterosexual and those guilty of indulging in homosexuality choose to do so and are selfish, perverted —and damned.

During these decades, reactions by Church leaders towards homosexuals has ranged from public ridicule to church courts leading to disfellowshipping, excommunication and, on occasion, to sanction by church leaders of physical violence against gay men.

In 2015, Mormon Church leaders banned all children being raised in homes headed by same-sex couples from being blessed and named as an infant, being baptized at age eight, or, for the boys, from being ordained to the priesthood at age twelve. These ordinances could only be performed when the child attained the age of eighteen and disavowed their parents' relationships. The children had to acknowledge that their parents were apostates. While this position has since been modified somewhat, the authorities retained the concept that same-gender marriage is apostasy.

A major portion of Part II, Promises, covers Caleb's experiences as a Mormon missionary. Mormon missionaries serve for two years, during which time they live a set-apart life, one quite different from Mormons in general, as well as from young adults in twenty-first-century America. Their behavior is strictly governed. They live with their companion twenty-four/seven; except when bathing or using the bathroom they are encouraged to be in the same room, including while sleeping.

They do not date anyone of the opposite sex, and should not be alone with a person of the opposite sex. They are restricted in their contacts with family, usually limited to one letter a week to parents and occasional letters to girlfriends. Regulations frequently restrict television viewing to LDS Church-sponsored programs and conferences. Radio, CDs, music videos, etc. usually fall outside of acceptable listening. Recreation is limited to one afternoon weekly when the elders frequently get together with other pairs of elders to play basketball; football is discouraged.

While writing *Legacies,* I have benefitted immensely from critiques offered by members of Writers' Workshop at Lutheran Church of Honolulu. Beyond helping me with clarity of events and dialogue among the characters, they suggested I add considerable explanation of Mormon experience for readers who do not know Mormonism intimately. Words dropped casually by characters in the novel can only be totally understood with this additional help. For this reason, I'm adding some basic information here and a

"Mormon Vocabulary," at the end of the novel.

Missionaries frequently invent words to express common experiences. The practice of walking through a neighborhood, knocking on the doors of homes to find people interested in hearing about the Mormon Church is called *tracting,* a term derived from the sharing of the pamphlets, or tracts, about the Prophet Joseph Smith or the Book of Mormon. Another common term among missionaries is *trunky,* referring to a missionary who is so longing for his release and return home that he has seemingly packed his suitcase—or trunk—preparatory to returning home. *Greenie* refers to a new missionary. *RM* is a returned missionary.

Apart from the missionary experience, terminology Mormons use frequently may confuse other people. In particular three terms about church polity used by Mormons vary in meaning from the traditional meaning among other Christians. One of these is *ward,* which in the secular world in the United States is a political district in a city; in Mormonism *ward* refers to the local congregation. Wards, or congregations, usually have a geographical basis, with the major exception being wards organized for language minorities. Members do not normally have the choice to attend a ward other than the one in which they live.

The leader of a ward is a bishop. A Mormon bishop has a similar status to a priest or pastor in various Christian congregations. Bishops choose two other men in the ward to serve as their counselors. The next higher level of organization in the Mormon Church is the *stake* which likewise has a geographical basis. Stakes usually contain between six and ten wards. The president of a stake is more akin in authority to a bishop in Protestant and Catholic churches. Leadership of stakes consists of a president, two counselors, and twelve other men making up a high council. These men have all received ordination as high priests.

Until the late 1960s, the only level of organization above the stake was the group of men called General Authorities: The First Presidency, the Quorum of Twelve Apostles, and the First Quorum of Seventy. These men are the only full-time callings in the Church; they hold their appointments until death. Given the growth of the Church in more recent times, the General Authorities have created an intermediary level to delegate the responsibilities to more men.

Although ordained, all these priesthood holders are in fact lay men; they have no professional training in theology, philosophy, psychology, or marriage or family counseling. Except for the General Authorities, they earn their living and support their families from whatever career they have chosen, be they farmers, laborers, teachers, doctors, lawyers, dentists, etc. In addition, they have limited terms in office. Bishops and their counselors usually serve for three years after which the stake president releases them and selects other men to fill the offices. Stake presidencies usually serve terms of five years after which they are released and replaced under the direction of the centralized church authorities.

Women do not hold the priesthood and cannot serve as ministers in the Mormon Church. Auxiliary organizations for women exist, somewhat parallel to the men's priesthood organizations. Adult women have a Relief Society organization within each ward and stake, presided over by a woman from the membership, called by the bishop for the ward Relief Society and by the stake president for the stake Relief Society. These sisters suggest names of women they would like to have as counselors who, if approved by the bishop or stake president, are then called by these priesthood leaders.

Previously known as the Young Women's Mutual Improvement Association, or YWMIA, Young Women is an organization for teenage girls. In the times of this novel, the YWMIA and the YMMIA met during the week as a weeknight youth activity. Currently Young Women meet on Sundays when the adult women have Relief Society and the men and boys over twelve have priesthood meetings. The bishop of each ward selects adult women to head the Young Women within each ward; the stake president selects leaders for the stake-wide Young Women.

The priesthood authority issues the callings, sets the women apart in their callings, and releases them. These priesthood leaders also call women to supervise the Primary, which is an auxiliary for children up to age twelve.

I have created a family tree of the characters in *Legacies*:

Part I The Corral

Sketch created by James Cartwright for this page,
September 2020

1
"Draper"

Six months after CT graduated from the "U" in the spring 1923, Mr. Reynolds told him that he was going to buy a small farmstead in Draper with CT's share of his mother's legacy. They would move together to Draper, and both could commute into the city on the Interurban—Mr. Reynolds to his post in a city government office and CT to his accounting job with Frank and Pearsall, obtained following graduation with a little help from "it's not what you know, but who." Mr. Reynolds was not against letting people know he had married Louisa Taylor.

"Why?" CT asked.

"Oh, we'll have a few chickens and a garden plot, maybe a beef calf for fattening. . ."

"Why? We've never farmed. You've never even grown a garden. Why?"

"I think a new environment would be good for you."

"Good for me? What's going on?"

"Maybe you should tell me."

"Tell you what?"

"You haven't gone to church for over a year. You spend your time with rowdies. Folks have told me they've seen you on Second South going into some of the speakeasies. And you spend a lot of time with that. . . that man."

"With who?" CT demanded, knowing his father didn't know Roger's name.

"Look, it's time you started to live up to the church's teachings. Your mother and I both come from stalwart pioneer

3

stock. You should be preserving your reputation."

"And what about Wilbur and Mary Elizabeth and Lucinda? They probably don't go to church either. The 'change of environment' to Chicago and San Francisco didn't make them active in the church."

"I don't care what you say, the decision's mine and the arrangements are made. I've had Mr. Boren find a place. He located two and I've already selected one. We move at the end of the year."

CT did not really take to the farm work with a great deal of enthusiasm. After a day of office work in the accounting firm, then a trip by the Interurban, he didn't relish feeding the chickens, gathering the eggs, and, the following summer after purchasing a steer, giving it some hay and grain and filling the water tub in his pen.

Weekends could be worse. Eventually, the chicken coop needed to

4

have the roosts scraped and the floor straw replaced. Chicken manure smells fairly strong if left to pile up for too long. Likewise the calf's roofed shelter over time accumulated a lot of manure. And, of course, CT had to drive to the feed store, buy and haul the hay, grains, and laying mash these animals consumed.

Towards the end of the summer, CT had the chore of finding a butcher to slaughter the calf and cut it up for storage. He found a meat company in nearby Sandy which had freezer space to rent to customers who didn't own home freezers—most people, in fact, in the south end of the county in the 1920s. He paid them to come to Draper, pick up the steer and haul it to their facility, slaughter it, cure it, cut it up, wrap it and freeze it. Mr. Snow, the butcher, wanted half the animal and five dollars a month freezer rental. CT had no idea if that was a good deal or not. He accepted and signed the agreement.

It was nice over the next few months to enjoy a roast of beef or good hamburger. In early spring, when he went to the meat locker, Mr. Snow asked if he wanted to buy another yearling calf that spring.

"I think I can find you a nice Hereford calf if you like."

"What's a Hereford?" CT asked.

"That's a good breed of beef cattle. Most people around here use Holstein steers 'cause they're available from all the dairies. But they don't make as good a beef animal. They're tall and lanky; Herefords are squat, broad shouldered, with shorter, thicker legs. More meat on them."

"Sure, I guess. I mean it's been good to have the beef we've had this winter. I guess I should ask how much it will cost before I commit."

"Tell you what. I'll locate the calf and if it costs too much for you, maybe we can make some kinda deal. I have customers here from cafes in Salt Lake

6

City who don't want dairy cattle, so I can sell any Hereford meat I get."

So, for his second summer in the country, CT would have a steer to feed and water.

During his first summer, he had learned that the steer would do better with grass to eat instead of just hay, and as they had a share of irrigation water with the property, he could convert the garden plot his father had not planted the previous year into an acre of pasture. Every six days and six hours, he could divert water from the main ditch into the pasture. If he planted pasture grass this summer, perhaps by late summer, the grass would be well established and he could turn the calf loose to graze. CT set to work on that project. He went next door to his neighbor.

"Mr. Carlson, I need some advice," CT began.

"Hey, CT. Name's Johnny. What can I do fer you?"

7

"I have learned that the calf will do better, grow fatter, with pasture grass than with hay. I'm wondering whether I could convert the large garden plot into pasture, then move the shed into the pasture."

"Sure."

"What do I need to do to prepare the land, make the pasture? What kind of seed do I buy? How do I build a ditch to irrigate it once it's planted?"

"Slow down. On the first Saturday after you send the calf to the butcher, I'll bring my tractor over and plow it up. You need to get all the stuff off the land first. I think you have some scraps from an old shed there. If you want the pen where you have the calf as part of your pasture, take down the fence. While I'm there, I'll plow you a ditch along the east end of the pasture. A week later, I'll come back to harrow the pasture. This'll make the rows where the irrigation water flows from your main ditch.

"You get the seed from the feed store. Get a blend with the main part bein' bluegrass and orchard grass, with some ryegrass and alfalfa and maybe some Timothy. Get perennials so you don't have to reseed every year. We'll plant it this fall about October depending on how cold September gets."

2
"Emma and Mary, Friends"

Draper was only five miles or so from the Interurban railroad between Provo and Salt Lake City, so it was much easier for Emma, a student at BYU, to get to Draper from Provo on the Interurban than to go to her home in Cedar Valley. For the year and a half Emma had been a student, she had been travelling to Draper on occasional weekends and for holidays, such as Thanksgiving and Easter. Aunt Mary, her father's much younger sister, always greeted her with joy. During these visits, the housework Emma and Aunt Mary shared sometimes separated them, such as when one scrubbed the kitchen floor and the other beat the carpets outside to clean them of accumulated dirt, but when they worked together, preparing, baking, and cooking the big Sunday dinners, they talked about almost everything.

"Well, dear, what are you doing for a social life?" Aunt Mary asked when Emma visited in early November.

"Oh, not a lot," Emma answered. "Jared, the boy in Goldbrickers, invited me to Homecoming dance. It was a lot of fun, but . . . I'm not really interested in him. Actually, I'm more attracted to Ben, one of his Goldbricker brothers. That doesn't look so good, does it?"

Aunt Mary chuckled. "You are loving being a socialite, aren't you?"

"Well, yes, there's no social life in Cedar Valley, so when I got to the 'Y,' I felt like a hungry girl in a pastry shop."

"Are you tasting all the pastries?"

"As many as invite me. But I can't just ask boys out on a date." Then noticing a look in Aunt Mary's eyes, she continued, "Well, my roommates and I could fix a Sunday dinner and invite some fellows over. I know, you didn't suggest that, but thanks for the idea."

"Oh, I get credit for the suggestion? Thank you. If you hadn't said it, I would have suggested it in a couple of seconds."

"The ladies in my social unit organize a couple of parties each quarter and the whole unit invites one of the men's social units. One time we invited the Tau Sigs who are mostly football players. We had a good time, but I'm not about to date any Tau Sigs I know. We ladies of Nautilus have a rivalry with one of the other sororities, so we each try to have the best parties and invite the most prestigious men's units. Sometimes it's a bit too much."

"What're the Goldbrickers like?"

"I understand they began as friends returning from the War. They decided to organize a group and felt the title of 'Goldbrickers' should fit them: you know, escape from any work you can in any way possible. Of course, by now, those men have all left, but the tradition carries on."

12

"How did you come up with the name 'Nautilus of NLU'?" Aunt Mary asked.

"Well, I didn't come up with the name. Our group existed for a few years before my time," Emma said, avoiding a clear answer to Aunt Mary's question.

"What does the name mean?" Aunt Mary persisted.

"Well . . ." Emma looked away. "We aren't supposed to tell anyone."

"You aren't? My goodness, are you trying to hide something," she quizzed, smiling with her eyes wide, affecting shock. "How naughty!"

After a short pause, Emma said, "You already know, don't you. Oh, you sly one. How did you find out?"

"Brig's cousin was one of the founding members, and she told me under similar pressure. I haven't told anyone

13

that I know. Except you. Please don't get her in trouble with the others."

"Of course, I won't. Do I know her?"

"I doubt it. She left the 'Y' to volunteer as a nurse's aide when we got into the War. Afterwards, she returned for a year or so. I don't know when she joined Nautilus."

After a short pause, Emma began another topic. "What's going on with Suzanne Fitzgerald? Is she going to get married to the man she liked?"

"Oh, that's over. She was quite the sorrowing maiden for a while, but she's now dating a man from Riverton, a Crane if I remember right."

"So, he must be related to us, or at least to our Butterfield relatives."

"I think only to the Butterfields."

14

"And Sharon Hazelton? How's she?"

"Oh dear, that one ended poorly. Sharon got pregnant and her father told her to leave. I'm not sure, but I think Brig managed to get her into a home in Salt Lake City. I don't know how much he knows about her now. I certainly cannot ask Brother or Sister Hazelton. I haven't asked Brig, so I cannot be a source of gossip among the ladies in the ward since I know nothing. It is pretty sad that Brother Hazelton turned her out. If she gives the baby up for adoption, she still has no place to go afterwards."

"Oh, that is sad."

3
"Two Families' Contrivances"

It wasn't a holiday, just two weeks before Thanksgiving in 1925, but Emma went to Draper because she knew Aunt Mary could use some help with preparations in advance of Thanksgiving —washing the table linens and ironing and starching them. That Sunday at church, she saw CT Reynolds.

"What can you tell me about CT and his father?" she asked Aunt Mary after Sunday School that day.

"I don't know much. They moved into the ward from Salt Lake City. I don't know why. Mr. Reynolds is a widower. His wife apparently was related to some of the leaders of the church, at least that's the impression he gives. His son— CT, isn't he?—doesn't seem to have any airs. They both work in the city, going in Mr. Reynold's car to the Interurban station. The two of them live alone in an old two-

16

room adobe on property Mr. Reynolds bought. They board with the Swansons, a neighboring family. I think they're building a house on the property."

"Oh, I know the Swansons."

"If you wish, we could invite the Reynolds to dinner some evening when you'll be here."

"Would that be a bother?"

"No. You help me prepare and it'll be fine. We'd better try for Tuesday evening; we have too much to do on Wednesday."

On their way back home, Mr. Reynolds commented to CT, "That was some fine young woman with the Rasmussens, You figure she's going to live here in Draper?"

"I have no idea. Knowing who she is might answer whether she'd consider moving here. Maybe she's married and her husband didn't come to church today."

"Yes, that's so," he said as if disinterested. "And it's nearly Thanksgiving, so she may have only come for the holiday." He fell silent, imagining how he might find out about the woman. *If she's related to the Rasmussens, maybe I can get them to invite us to supper some night before Thanksgiving itself,* he thought.

It didn't take Mr. Reynolds long to find an opportunity to speak with Brigham Rasmussen. He had already purchased the coal he and CT would need to heat their house for the winter, and the check had cleared the bank. Mr. Reynolds merely decided to stop at the coal company weighing house to make certain.

"Good afternoon, Bishop Rasmussen. I could not remember if my check to you cleared the bank or not. I certainly hope there was no problem."

18

"I'll look it up right now, Brother Reynolds." It took a minute for Brigham Rasmussen to retrieve the ledger and look up the payment. "Yes, we sent it in the end of September. He glanced down at another page of his ledger. "It isn't in our file of returned checks, so yes, we have the money. Thanks for asking."

"That was a fine-looking young woman with you on Sunday. Is she a relative?"

"She's our niece, Emma, daughter of Mary's brother, Reuben. He ranches out in Cedar Valley. Emma's attending the 'Y' and comes here for some weekends. It's much more convenient to get here on the Interurban than to make the long trip back to Cedar Valley."

That sounded sufficient for Mr. Reynolds. *There are no socially outstanding families in Draper; the Rasmussens are among the leading families—though, of course, they would not amount to much in Salt Lake City. Nevertheless, the young Rasmussen*

19

woman would be as good as one could
expect in Draper. He left the office.

Mr. Reynolds believed his efforts made all the difference. Two evenings later, Brigham Rasmussen drove his delivery truck by the Reynolds' house on his way home after making a delivery in the neighborhood.

"Mary and I would like to invite you and your son to supper on Tuesday evening before Thanksgiving," Brigham said to Mr. Reynolds at the door.

"We thank you," answered Mr. Reynolds. "Will your niece be there? It'd be a pleasure to meet her."

"I think she may be back by then. She is planning to spend the Thanksgiving weekend here, but I'm not certain she will come on Tuesday. Mary, however, has her hands full on Wednesday getting ready for Thanksgiving."

"We'll be honored to accept, and, of course, we'd love to meet your niece."

After Bishop Rasmussen left, Mr. Reynolds informed CT of the invitation. "Please make certain you make the 5:15 train that night or we will be awfully late."

Why would the Rasmussens invite us to supper now? CT wondered. *We've lived here for months. Nobody else has invited us.* Nor, of course, had they invited anyone to their place. They were, after all, two single men living together in a shack, without a housekeeper, cook, or anyone to do domestic work. How could they host anyone?

On Tuesday evening, after returning from work, Mr. Reynolds and CT dressed for dinner and then drove Mr. Reynold's car to the Rasmussen home. They parked in front of the small, white, wooden frame house just west of the coal business. When they knocked on the front door, Emma, smiling, opened the door. She invited them in.

The courtship of CT and Emma, begun that November evening, continued over the occasional weekends when Emma could come from Provo.

4
"Courtship"

There was not a lot to do in
Draper of a social nature apart from ward
activities. One Saturday night in early
February, CT borrowed Mr. Reynolds' car
and drove with Emma into Salt Lake City
to attend the University of Utah–BYU
basketball game at Einar Nielsen
Fieldhouse on the "U" campus. Of course,
most of the attendees were Utah fans, so
Emma's cheers for the "Y" were quite
isolated amid the roar coming from the
Utah crowd. Afterwards CT and Emma
joined two other couples, CT's frat
brothers and their dates, for hamburgers
and spirited conversation about the game.
That night it was quite late when CT and
Emma finally got back to Draper.

Though he would have gladly
slept in the next day, CT felt he had to be
in church that morning. He got up early,
fed the animals, milked the cow, washed
up and shaved. Mr. Reynolds decidedly

approved of CT's reformation. *If CT attends church because of Emma even after such a late night, she is a good influence on him. Maybe he might become safe here in Draper.*

In April, CT took Emma to the Phi Delta Theta fraternity's spring formal at the Hotel Newhouse on Fourth South and Main Street in Salt Lake City. As several of the fraternity alumni attended, CT had friends there to whom he introduced Emma. By the end of that evening, everyone at the dance knew CT and Emma would be married the following autumn.

In June, Emma's father promised them three ewes as his wedding gift plus the promise that he would have them bred with his rams each autumn so they could raise lambs for their meat locker. He would deliver them to Emma and CT when he brought the sheep from the summer range in the Uintah Mountains down through Provo Canyon on the way to Cedar Valley.

24

In September, they married in the Salt Lake Temple. The small group for the ceremony included Mr. Reynolds and three of CT's aunts and uncles, relieved both because CT was finally getting married and because the wedding was in the Temple. Of course, Aunt Mary and Uncle Brigham and Emma's father attended as well. No one else came to the Temple ceremony.

A reception for the newlyweds took place that night in the Roundhouse behind the Draper Ward church. The next day, CT and Emma caught the Western Pacific train from Salt Lake City to San Francisco for their honeymoon.

5
"Swimming"

In 1921, five years before CT and Emma married, CT met Roger. Second South Street in Salt Lake City was just far enough away from the Gentile center of business along Exchange Place and Main Street between Third and Fourth South that it could entice some people from the Mormon end, yet it was far enough from South Temple to be quite free of tight Mormon control. Several of the buildings throughout this buffer-zone business district had basement levels where cafes, pawn shops, bargain retail stores could be reached by a short flight of steps down from the street. Along Second South Street, a few clandestine bars existed, "hidden" during Prohibition.

The night he met Roger in mid-October, CT went to Victor's, one of these bars. He strutted down the stairs from the street that night as if saying, 'Yeah, I'm goin' to a speakeasy on Second

South. So what?' There was a large crowd that weekend night, and he knew some of his frat brothers would be there. When he saw Roger, however, CT paused and stared. Roger seemed aware that he was a subject of interest. He turned his head toward CT. Their eyes met and held. CT blushed and turned away. He began looking for his frat brothers.

Two minutes later, he heard a voice to his side, "Hi, I'm Roger."

Turning, CT found himself looking into the man's eyes. "Uh, I'm CT…. I, uh, I think I've seen you at the 'U,' no?"

"Sure thing. Maybe in Einar Nielsen. I work there passing out towels in the men's dressing room."

"You must be on some team or another."

"Yeah. I swim on the varsity. And you?"

"Oh, I don't swim. I'd sink. I run sprints on the track team. I can run for the 'U,' but I can't swim. I understand they probably won't let me graduate 'cause I can't swim."

"I'll bet I could teach you."

"Oh, no! Not me. I really don't swim."

"Hey, what can you lose? Let me try. Where do you live?"

"I live with my father on Harvard Street, 1125. But I'm almost always at the Phi Delt house."

"Look, I'll pick you up Monday night at eight o'clock at Phi Delt and we'll go to Deseret Gym. I have keys 'cause I coach there; it's completely legit. There won't be any swimmers there by that time and we'll use the shallow end of the pool. If I can't have you ready to pass the swimming test by end of next quarter, I'll treat you and your date to the finest meal in the city. We'll go to the gym

28

every Monday and Thursday night and swim."

"You're on," CT agreed. Over the next two days, whenever he thought about Monday night, he wasn't so sure he should have accepted. He was sure he couldn't learn to swim; he'd probably drown before enjoying any dinner.

Determined to teach CT how to swim, Roger led him to the shallow end of the pool that following Monday night. He began by showing CT how his own head and chest always stayed near the surface since he had air in his lungs and he didn't panic. Even when he turned face down, he showed CT that his head was always near the surface. To breathe all he needed to do was tilt his head back, bringing his face out of the water.

Then Roger stood on CT's left side facing him. He put his right hand on CT's back between CT's shoulder blades. "Now lean back against my hand. I will hold you. Lean back and relax."

Roger shifted his right leg out, so, as CT leaned back, Roger would still be even with CT's torso and he would be able to hold him. Roger then placed his left hand firmly under the small of CT's back. Although his weight was still supported by Roger, CT was floating.

"Breathe in. Exhale. Inhale. Keep it regular. Relax. Softer, softer. You don't need to gulp all the air in the universe. Easy. Inhale, exhale. Inhale, exhale. Slowly, stay relaxed, breathe naturally. You're safe."

"Okay, stand up. I want to show you something else," Roger instructed, helping CT back to a standing position. "Now watch carefully."

Roger then lay face down in the water, not moving, his entire face submerged in water. Finally, he tilted his head back, bringing his face out of the water, and inhaled before lowering his head until his face was once again submerged. He lay there, holding still, slowly exhaling air. A minute went by.

"Hey! Come up," CT said, louder than usual. Roger finally lifted his head, inhaled, and returned his face into the water. He slowly exhaled the air in his lungs, creating bubbles on both sides of his head. After exhaling the air, another minute and a half or so, Roger stood up.

"See, even without doing anything, I floated close enough to the surface to lift my face out of the water and get some air. There's so much air in your lungs—in everyone's lungs—that you'll float. Your legs and feet will sink downward, but the air in your lungs will keep you near the surface. My feet never touched the floor and we're only in water three feet deep.

"Lean forward onto my left hand," Roger told CT. "I'll provide you the support, but we are taking you down until your face is entirely under water."

Roger stepped to his left, then took a second step to lower CT further into the water. When CT's nose hit the water, he jerked upright. "Augh."

31

"Hey, I've got you. My hand was under your chest. I'll be holding you up. Now try again. Lean forward onto my hand. Let's go. Keep leaning down. Further." Roger took small steps to his left, lowering CT further into the water. He stopped just before submerging CT's face.

"Relax. We're going further down. Take a breath. Hold it while I count to five, then slowly let it out while I count to five. Don't let it all out until I reach five the second time. Ready. Inhale. Down we go. One, two, three, four, five. Now slowly exhale. One, two, three. . ."

"God! I can't do it," CT shouted, standing up and throwing out his arms, striking Roger's flank. "I'll drown."

"Hey, man. You did it for the count of three. Let the air out slower and you'll be fine. Now let's try again."

I want to climb out, now! I want this over, done with. He knew, however, if he quit, he couldn't ever face Roger

32

again. And he definitely wanted to see him again. *Maybe Roger will tell others as well.*

CT leaned forward again onto Roger's hand.

"Now remember. Exhale slowly, a full count to five."

CT leaned forward and Roger lowered him into the water. "Inhale," he said just before lowering CT's face under the surface. "One, two, three, four, five. Now exhale slowly. One, two, three, four, five. Great," he said lifting CT's chest and face out of the water. "We're going again."

"No. Wait. I'm still out of breath!"

When Roger stopped lowering his hand, CT quit trying to stand up and relaxed some.

"Ready? Here we go," Roger said, lowering his hand and letting CT's chest and then face back down into the water.

Roger repeated the drill two more times without CT having any problem.

"Now this time, I'm not going to lift you up. You tip your head back after you exhale to bring your face out of the water. Inhale, then tuck your face back under the water and exhale. When you are out of air again, lift your face out of the water and inhale. I'll count; keep your face under for the count of five each time while you exhale, then a quick inhale and return to the water."

CT lowered his face into the water, exhaled to Roger's count, lifted his face, gulped air, and returned his face to the water, but then began flailing his arms and gasping. Roger lifted him up and held him upright.

"What happened?" he asked.

When he could, CT explained. "I got water in my nose and throat. I knew I would drown."

"No, you won't. I won't let you drown. That'd be bad form." Roger smiled. "I should have explained. Inhale through your mouth, but close it before you put your face under. Exhale through your nose. Are you okay now?"

After doing this drill a couple of times successfully, Roger took CT to the edge of the pool where they stood about waist deep. Holding his left arm out in front of him and holding onto the gutter, Roger showed CT how to put his head in the water, tilting his head back so his face was looking ahead.

"With your head tilted up, your nose will rise further out of the water when you turn to the side to breathe in. Now watch." Roger lowered his face into the water, tipping his head; he turned his head to his right so his face was out of the water. He inhaled through his mouth, turned his face into the water and exhaled through his nose, then turned his head again, bringing his face out of the water and inhaled.

"Now you do it. Look right so your face is out of the water but put your head further down, into the water. Yeah. Inhale, turn your face into the water and exhale. Turn your face back to the side. Inhale through your mouth. Close your mouth; exhale through your nose.

"This is the base for our next lesson on Thursday. You've done real good," Roger said, putting his arm around CT's shoulder and squeezing it. "Let's go shower."

CT was thrilled.

In the second session, Thursday night, Roger began everything all over again, starting as he did the first night. After they worked at the side with the breathing, Roger showed CT the next step. He held onto the gutter with his left hand and put his right hand against the pool wall about a foot below the surface. Then he pushed his torso and legs away from the wall and began to kick while he practiced the breathing exercise.

"Now you do it."

CT held onto the gutter with his left hand and put his right hand down against the wall of the pool below the surface of the water. He actually got his feet off the floor of the pool and began kicking wildly, but he wouldn't put his face into the water.

"Let's go back a bit. Place your hands in these same positions, but keep standing on the floor. Now let's practice the breathing again. Slow, easy. Turn, inhale. Turn, exhale. Turn, inhale through your mouth; turn exhale through your nose. Inhale, exhale. Inhale, exhale. Remember to inhale through your mouth. Close your mouth under water and exhale through your nose. You're doing fine."

By the end of the third session, Roger had CT kicking and breathing fairly evenly. CT knew now he would not drown. The fourth session Roger showed CT the back stroke, a swimming stroke where CT's face was almost always out of the water; breathing would not be as

37

much of a challenge. CT's main challenge with the backstroke occurred as he would bend his knees to prepare for the kick and simultaneously bring his hands up towards his chest for the arm stroke; then his body tended to sink into the water. More than once, CT stood up, panicked.

"Remember you're not going to sink. Even when your face is under water, it's within inches of air. Just relax. Now try it again."

In the fifth session after a review, Roger showed CT the basics of the breast stroke. CT's major challenge on this stroke was to put his face entirely under water except to look up to inhale air. By the end of this session, CT could do it, gulping in air and blowing it all out with every stroke. It wasn't elegant, nor good form, but it was swimming. For the next few sessions, Roger worked on getting CT to breathe more slowly, to be more relaxed, to lessen his fear of running out of air.

"Don't blow out all your air on each stroke. Try doing two complete strokes without inhaling more air."

"Tonight," Roger told CT at the beginning of the eighth session, "you have a mid-term. You're going to swim any stroke you wish for ten minutes without stopping, no standing on the bottom, no holding onto the side. Just keep going." After successfully completing the exam, CT and Roger relaxed a short time.

"This is a short session," CT said.

"Oh no," Roger answered. "Now I'm going to teach you the most efficient stroke. Once you've learned it, you'll prefer it to the others because you can swim faster using this stroke than the other strokes you've learned. It's called the crawl. Watch."

After briefly demonstrating the crawl, Roger explained the stroke pattern. "As you pull your right arm, elbow first, out of the water, roll your body slightly to your left, bringing your face mostly out of the water. Inhale through your mouth as you continue raising and straightening your arm over your head. As you slide your hand and arm back into the water, your body will rotate slightly back, putting your face back under the water. Begin exhaling slowly through your nose. Exhale slowly enough that you do not need to inhale until your right arm is against your leg and ready to come out of the water again."

At the end of the session, Roger asked, "Ready to register for swimming? You have to take the course to prove you can swim."

"You did it! I didn't think you could, but you've taught me to swim." CT grabbed Roger into a bear hug.

Roger hugged CT, "We'll continue to meet each Monday and Thursday, keep practicing. You'll do great in class."

6
"CT the Builder, 1926"

Over five years later, CT faced a
challenge, similar to his learning to swim,
that would be difficult and last over
several months. The challenge involved
his learning to become a farmer of sorts; it
became earnest with construction of a
shed and corral to shelter some sheep, but
it started with Reuben's announcement in
June of his wedding gift to Emma and
CT: three ewes and an older ram from his
flock. At first, raising sheep seemed easy,
certainly less terrifying than learning to
swim had been, but as he learned more, he
began to see the challenges. Early, he
turned to Johnny Carlson.

"Help, please," CT implored when
Johnny opened the door to his house.

"What's goin' on?" Johnny asked.

"Emma's father's giving us some
sheep so we can have lambs every year

41

for the locker, and he says we need a shed to shelter them during the winter and at lambing time. Do you have any idea where I can buy one for not too much money?"

"Hey, you an' me can build one for less than you'd spend buying one and getting it delivered here. What size do you need?"

"I don't know. We'll have three sheep, well four, with the ram."

"Well, we can build a shed that'll shelter four or five sheep easily. I'll work on some plans for you. Come back Sunday afternoon and I'll show you what I've come up with."

On Sunday, Johnny indeed had some plans, plans which called for quite a bit of work.

"I think we should move the fence of the pasture to include the chicken coop and the feed shed so they can be next to the shelter for the sheep. And I think we

42

should build a corral just outside the shed. It'll be handy as a smaller pen when you don't want them loose in the pasture. We'll build a stanchion and trusses on the two sides supporting a crossbeam. We can put tackle on the crossbeam where you hang the animal carcass and slaughter the animals right there."

"I am *not* going to slaughter the animals here," CT said.

"Oh, you won't have to do it yourself, but you'll save time and money if you can have the slaughtering done here. You won't have to pay to have the animals hauled to the locker in Sandy or some other place. The butcher in Sandy would probably be willing to come here to slaughter the animals, then haul the meat to the lockers."

So, CT was persuaded.

The following Sunday after dinner, CT went next door to Johnny's house to plan the first part of the project, moving the pasture fence to include the outbuildings they already had built; they would build the sheep pen next to the chicken coop on the inside of the enlarged pasture. CT and Johnny decided when to shop for necessary materials so they might install the additional fencing the following Saturday. A week later, they mixed cement and poured a foundation and floor for the shed, including anchoring corner posts, wall studs, and posts for a doorway. For the next month or so, in the evenings after returning from work, CT nailed siding boards onto the studs and corner posts. By the end of July, they had finished the shed.

Next came the big project: the corral. Johnny's plans called for corner posts, two gates, and stanchions on two opposite sides to hold a crossbeam. Three 2x6 boards running horizontally would create the sides of the corral with about a foot between each. The heavy 2x6 boards required they work together, primarily on Saturdays and Sundays, but they also got some work done on week nights. Always both men were tired from the hard work.

One evening in mid-September, right before he and Emma married, after a particularly hard day at work, CT and Johnny were nailing boards onto corner posts of the yet unfinished corral. CT was exhausted and discouraged.

As he drove Emma back to Aunt Mary and Uncle Brigham's for the night, CT complained to Emma, "I had no idea that damned corral could take so long or be so hard to build. Why didn't Johnny warn me. God, I'm sick of it."

Construction of the corral took over nine weeks, interrupted at times by CT's preparations for the wedding and the honeymoon to follow. Before they finished, Emma's father brought his sheep down for the winter range. At Lehi, he left the herd in the charge of the Basque herders and hauled the ewes and an older ram in his pickup truck up to Draper. He said he would leave this ram with Emma and CT until Thanksgiving, if he could make it up to Draper then.

"Finally. It's done," CT exclaimed to Emma the night after they completed the corral. "I don't feel much like an accountant anymore. But I'm certainly not cut out to be a construction worker!" Three days later, CT realized with pride how nicely the coral and shed provided for the sheep. It was just a quiet revelation, not accompanying any event of significance. This realization accompanied his remembrance of the triumph he felt when Roger taught him to swim. Remembering that, he realized again how much he wanted to reconnect.

7
"Lambs and Mr. Reynolds"

In early 1927, CT and Emma agreed that every evening she would pen the ewes about four o'clock before he arrived back to Draper from his work as an accountant in town. If it was not stormy, CT would let them out into the pasture in the morning before going to work. That way the sheep would have shelter when they began to lamb.

One morning about 5:00 AM, he opened the door into the shed and saw one of the young ewes had dropped a lamb, which was lying in the corner of the shed, ignored by the ewe, standing with the bloody afterbirth still suspended from her. CT left, shutting the door carefully. On his way to get Emma, nausea gripped him. After recovering, he ran to the house to tell Emma.

Emma removed from the wood stove the pans she was using to cook breakfast, then the two of them went back to the shed where they saw that an older ewe had given birth. Unlike the first ewe, she was standing over it, licking it clean and encouraging it to stand. Once the lamb was teetering on its own, the ewe turned to her own afterbirth lying near the lamb and began licking it up. Once more, CT gagged.

When CT gagged, Emma softly explained, "CT, it's natural. She needs to do this to begin lactating and, if her lamb had been born in the wild, eating the afterbirth removes any scent of blood. Keeps the coyotes away. They wouldn't survive unless they ate it."

Emma looked across the shed to where the first lamb lay. "Looks like we lost the first one."

"I'll take it out and bury it in the pasture."

"Yes, right away, at least two feet deep. Even dogs can be a problem. Looks like the third ewe is going into labor already. . . and, oh, yes, this young one is delivering another lamb. Maybe she will take to this one. They usually do drop two."

CT lifted the dead lamb and the straw under it with a pitchfork and carried it out into the pasture. He retrieved a shovel from the tool room. In the early dawn, he heard a dog baying. *Yes, I need to get this done quickly.*

When he returned to the shed after burying the dead lamb, the third ewe had dropped a lamb and was licking it clean while also trying to lick up her afterbirth which still clung to her. The young ewe who had lost her lamb was clearly in labor again. They had their hands full this morning; CT realized he would obviously be late for work at Frank and Pearsall, Accountants.

"Perhaps," he said to Emma, "father would be willing to stop at the firm and tell them I won't be in this morning. Maybe I can make it in this afternoon."

"Oh, your father's breakfast will be ruined," Emma cried. "I have to get back to the kitchen." She looked to CT, noticing his look of insecurity with the birthing. "There isn't much anyone can do, but watch to see if there's any problem. Don't touch any of the lambs until after they are up and nursing; our scent will likely cause the ewe to abandon the lamb. If the afterbirth doesn't drop on its own, pull it gently away and then allow the ewe to eat it. She will know her own afterbirth by scent, you won't have to push it to her. . . Oh dear, your father will be irate."

"Oh, I think he will understand."

On the morning the ewes lambed, Mr. Reynolds got up at his usual time. Immediately he noticed the quiet within the house; no one was making breakfast in the kitchen downstairs. He kept to his normal morning routine. He went into the bathroom, filled the basin with water, soaped his face and rinsed it, then lathered his face with his shaving brush. Partway through stropping his straight edge, he

50

paused, listening for any sounds of breakfast preparations. Nothing. "Well, I'm not responsible for rousing that woman up," he muttered aloud.

He finished his shaving ritual and returned to his bedroom to dress for work. He walked downstairs, through the dining room and into the kitchen. No one was there, the fire in the stove was dwindling, the frying pan and eggs sitting on a side board.

Emma returned to the house, dreading the scene to come.

"What in heaven's name have you been doing?" Mr. Reynolds demanded when she stepped into the kitchen.

"The ewes have begun to lamb and we've lots of work to do."

"Well, here I'm waiting for my breakfast and now I'm going to be late to work. If this is breakfast," he said, pointing to the pans, "you will have to start over. I won't eat cold bacon and eggs. This is absolutely unacceptable."

She emptied the frying pans onto a plate and returned the pans to the stove. She could immediately see that the fire had died way down, and she would have to refuel it and wait for it to heat. She removed a pan to access the grate. After putting wood on the fire, she set the pan back on the stove top to heat, then sliced more bread for toasting, and retrieved two eggs from the ice box. The new strips of bacon in the first pan began to sizzle; soon the pan would be hot enough for the eggs.

"How would you like your eggs this morning," she asked tentatively.

"I always want them over easy," he answered.

She remembered one morning the previous week he asked the eggs be scrambled, but she didn't say anything.

52

"I absolutely must leave in fifteen minutes. I don't suppose CT is anywhere near ready to go. I can't wait; he'll have to get to the Interurban some other way."

In the meantime, Emma toasted the bread slices and cracked two eggs into the hot pan with some drippings. She knew the pan was too hot, and the eggs would either stick or cook too hard. They did, and she broke the yoke of one as she turned it over. She placed bacon strips on a plate with the toast and eggs and placed it on the table.

"This bacon isn't done enough. You trying to poison me with trichinosis?" Then after cutting his fork into one of the eggs, he added, "The eggs are overdone, They're hard, almost inedible."

CT entered the kitchen, and Mr. Reynolds turned to him. "I am leaving in ten minutes and will not wait for you. I hope you will find some other way to the Interurban station."

"Please stop at Frank and Pearsall and tell them I cannot make it in this morning but will be there by noon if possible."

"That will make me a full ten minutes later. I guess I have to tell them, to save you your job. I certainly don't want to be the cause of your throwing away a good career. Do try to get there this afternoon."

Mr. Reynolds left the kitchen to finish his toiletries and prepare to leave for work.

"Well, what's the latest in the lambing shed?" Emma asked.

"The young ewe took care of her second one okay. One of the older ewes is going to have triplets, though the last one hasn't come out yet. The other ewe has twins and it looks like that's it for her. God, I'm exhausted."

"Go take a nice bath. You'll feel much better after you get all this cleaned

54

off. I'll quickly check on the ewes and then get your breakfast ready."

Mr. Reynolds walked through the kitchen without speaking to either Emma or CT and out the door. He got into his car and drove to the Interurban station.

8
"Oysters and Tails"

Shortly after the lambing, Emma informed CT that they needed to call a veterinarian to have the lambs docked and the male lambs castrated. She suggested Dr. Anderson in Utah Valley, who doctored her father's sheep when needed. CT found his telephone number, and one night, on his way home from work, he stopped at the seed store in Draper to use the pay telephone. Dr. Anderson said he could come to the Draper farm on Saturday, a week and a half after the lambing.

On that Saturday morning, CT answered Dr. Anderson's knock on the kitchen door. "You must be Dr. Anderson. Come in. I'll get my coat and be right with you."

"Good morning, Doc," Emma smiled, turning away from the sink where she had been washing up the dishes.

"Good morning, Emma. It's good to see you. I suppose the last time I saw you was about a year ago out in Cedar Valley for this same job."

"Yes, if you've gone out there since then, I was up here."

"By the way, you want the oysters?"

"Sure," she responded. "I'll get you a pan to put them in."

Just then CT returned with his coat. Emma handed the doctor a pan, and the two men walked out the door.

Earlier that morning, CT had corralled the ewes and lambs by bribing the ewes with a little grain. Trapped in the corral, the lambs were easily caught. The doctor, kneeling on the ground in the corral, asked CT to bring him the lambs one at a time. CT held the lambs while Dr. Anderson docked them with large pincers. He cut the tails off as close to their bodies as he could.

"Why cut their tails off?" CT asked, wincing at what he thought must be quite painful for the lambs.

"The tails are useless and they're really health hazards. They collect dung that leads to insect infestation as well as stops their elimination if it gets too bad. If you keep the lamb for breeding, then you have to shear the wool off the next spring. The tail is so thin it takes a lot of time to shear it and the wool from it is so filled with dried dung as to be relatively worthless. So, to save time and effort, we dock the lambs near birth."

"Oh," CT whispered.

"Okay, now we castrate the males," Dr. Anderson said when the final lamb had been docked. "So, you want the oysters?"

"Oysters?" CT looked puzzled.

"Bring me one of the male lambs." CT caught one and carried it to the doctor. "Lay him down on his side with his legs toward me. You kneel down next to the lamb's back facing me."

"Hand me the cutting tool. . . No, no wait. I've already got it," Dr. Anderson said. He smiled, thinking of CT's confusion and Emma's quick answer to his question back in the kitchen.

"Hold him down with your hand on his neck. No, use your other hand; you'll need that hand to hold up his hind leg." CT placed his left hand on the neck and shoulder of the lamb, keeping the lamb down, and with his right hand he held the lamb's right leg up exposing his scrotum to the doctor.

Dr. Anderson had clear access to the lamb's testicles. He quickly cut the testicles off without cutting the lamb unnecessarily.

Dr. Anderson dropped the testicles into the pan, grasped a small bottle of disinfectant and poured some over the lamb's wound. It happened so fast, from capture through disinfectant, that the lamb

59

hardly bleated. CT released the lamb, then rose to catch the other male lamb, but staggered. After a short pause, CT went over to the other male lamb, picked him up, and brought him to the doctor, who performed the same action. Smiling again, Dr. Anderson wondered whether Emma was planning on sharing her delicacy.

"There," Dr. Anderson stood up and put the cutter back in his toolbox. "You can let them all out now. Check the lambs every night and morning for the next few days to make sure no infection gets started on their tails or scrotal sacks."

As CT went to the corral gate to let the sheep loose, Dr. Anderson picked up the pan. "You can throw the tails away. Make sure the sheep are calm after they go out," he said, to keep CT distracted while he walked to the kitchen to give the pan to Emma.

When CT arrived back at the kitchen, Dr. Anderson asked if the sheep were okay. "Yes, they seem fine. Will a check be okay?" he asked, walking to the utility drawer.

"That'll do fine."

That evening Emma prepared fried chicken for dinner and had a side dish of some small meatballs. "I don't know if you want this," she offered CT. "We call them Rocky Mountain oysters. They really taste good and are very tender." She placed two on her plate, leaving two for CT. He blanched.

9
"Holidays"

Two years after CT and Emma married, Mr. Reynolds notified the renters who lived in his home in the city that he would be returning to live in Salt Lake City, and they would have to find another place to live.

Now that CT is married and adjusted to the country, Mr. Reynolds reasoned, *he has an anchor in Draper. He won't move back to the city. Although he doesn't attend church as much as he should, he seems to fit in with the townspeople . . . of course they still treat us as outsiders.*

"They're all equals," Mr. Reynolds said softly about Emma and the people in Draper. "CT never did value the family heritage as much as he should. He didn't appreciate his mother's being a Taylor nor the fact that both sets of his grandparents crossed the plains as pioneers to the Valley. Well, I can't cure that. He's twenty-eight. If he doesn't appreciate our heritage by now, it's not going to happen. As for me, I'm not cut out for country living."

"Freedom, Glorious freedom!" Emma, could not help rejoicing aloud.

She had known early on that Mr. Reynolds did not approve of her. On various occasions, he repeated that the Reynolds were among the best of Salt Lake City society; they had married into the leading families of the Church, such as the Taylors; and, of course, they were superior in conduct and manners to most of the people living in Draper, including, of course, Emma and her extended family. He even said CT had married beneath himself. On a few occasions he made such comments while others were within hearing distance.

He frequently said cutting personal comments to Emma. She seldom cooked well enough for him. She did not iron his shirts properly. She didn't dust his room sufficiently or misplaced his personal items when she cleaned. "Did you learn anything by reading in my journal," he snapped one day.

Now she found herself anticipating the upcoming holidays. After Mr. Reynolds returned to Salt Lake City, Emma invited Aunt Mary and Uncle Brigham and their children to their home for Thanksgiving. She confided to Aunt Mary how delighted she felt these last two months planning to have her home just to CT and herself. "It has been impossible to please him, *ever*," she said.

Emma enjoyed November. She planned which table linens she would use; washed them carefully, then starched and ironed them. She unwrapped and washed CT's mother's china, which had been stored when Mr. Reynolds lived with them. As CT was the only one of his children to marry, he had given it to CT and Emma as a wedding gift, but Mr. Reynolds didn't want to use it after his wife's death so it had been packed away. Emma carefully placed all the plates and

64

bowls in a china cupboard. She brought out the silver place settings, also from CT's family, polished every piece, and restored it to the case where it was protected from tarnishing. One afternoon in the week before Thanksgiving, she hiked into the foothills to cut some leaves from scrub oak and maple for a table setting.

About a week before Thanksgiving Emma asked Aunt Mary how to roast the turkey and how to prepare a delicious stuffing. On Thursday of that week she went to the butcher's in Sandy and discovered that she could buy a turkey and pick it up on Wednesday before Thanksgiving. Aunt Mary promised she would bring pies and roasted squash, which was a huge relief. Emma had never baked pies, breads, or pastries as her father had always hired a cook.

Thanksgiving Day began early in the morning, at 4:30 instead of the usual 5:00 o'clock. First job, she remembered, was to build a fire in the oven. Then retrieving the turkey from the ice box in the back room behind the kitchen, she rubbed it down with sage, salt, pepper, stuffed it with the dressing she had prepared the night before, and placed it in the oven.

From root vegetables saved during fall harvest, she selected carrots, potatoes, onions, and parsnips. These she cut up into large pieces and placed on baking dishes with dabs of butter, salt, pepper, adding brown sugar to the seasoning on the carrots. By the time Aunt Mary and Uncle Brigham arrived in the late morning, Emma was ready for a nap.

CT and Uncle Brigham retired to the living room to enjoy the fire in the fireplace and listen to the radio account of the Utah State Agricultural College–University of Utah football game. The children played board games on the living room floor. Aunt Mary and Emma continued to prepare the meal, setting hot dishes on the table as they finished cooking.

66

Preparing the meal was hard work but worth it. Everyone enjoyed Emma's first Thanksgiving feast. The turkey was tender and delicious, especially the dark meat. The dressing was savory. All the side dishes were very tasty. As the serving platters were emptied, there were many sighs of satisfaction. Emma blushed and smiled at the compliments.

Thanksgiving night, Emma shared with CT the plans she had made for Christmas. "I think we should have a family custom of having Christmas Eve together as a family in our own home, especially after children come."

"That sounds good," CT responded.

"I'll fix whatever you wish for supper that night. We could have a leg of lamb, or one of the roasts of beef. We could even have a ham, if you like; Uncle Brigham gave us two hams from the shoats he slaughtered this fall."

"I'm sure I'll have at least part of the day off," CT said. "I'll try to bring home a tree and decorate it. After dinner, we can light it and sit by the fire."

"I think we should read the story of the first Christmas in Luke. Will you read it?"

"Sure," CT agreed. "I'll try to read it over beforehand, so I can do it right."

"Oh, you'll read beautifully," she laughed. "You always do."

In the weeks following Thanksgiving, listening to CT rehearsing his reading of the Christmas story in Luke, Emma decided she would also prepare a reading. She selected the children's poem, "'Twas the Night Before Christmas." Emma practiced her reading while CT was at work, so her contribution would be a surprise.

On Christmas Eve, CT arrived home from Salt Lake City at two o'clock. He brought with him a small piñon pine

68

he was able to buy from a garden store in the city. He put it into a bucket of water and figured out how to stabilize it in the bucket so it wouldn't tip over when placed in the living room.

After getting the tree set up, he strung electric lights on it. Then he placed red ornaments on the branches. When he plugged in the lights, a rather large patch without lights revealed that CT was still a novice in Christmas tree decorating. Immediately he unplugged the lights and tried moving around some of the lights, but after ornaments are on the tree, moving strings of lights is always difficult. CT decided that the tree was finished.

In the meantime, the pungent scent of piñon filled the house. "I can't resist," Emma said, coming into the living room. "It smells so good. I'm sorry, I know I'm supposed to stay out of the living room so it can be a surprise."

"I don't know. I think Santa's going to say this misbehavior will cost you," CT smiled, gathering her into his arms and kissing her softly. They stood, CT holding Emma for a minute or so, then he looked down at her and asked, "When will dinner be ready? I should shower beforehand."

"Oh, I need to get back to the kitchen. I think about five o'clock."

CT gathered up the boxes in which they had stored the colored balls and the strings of lights and took them, along with the tools he had used to stabilize the tree, back to the storeroom.

After his shower and dressing, he came from the shower at the back of the house into the kitchen. Emma was in the process of moving the ham from the rack on which she had roasted it to a large china platter to take to the dining room.

"I'll carry that," CT said. "After you." She picked up one more bowl of food and preceded CT into the dining room. Emma had set the table for two with bayberry candles lit. They sat, CT

70

took Emma's hands in his and offered a prayer to bless the food and give thanks for the beautiful, sacred night.

"This ham is delicious," CT said. "And the squash is too. And you know I don't usually like vegetables."

Emma glowed.

When they finished Christmas Eve dinner, CT said, "Let me help you with the dishes before we go into the living room and the fire. Then we can go from there to bed without having to do chores."

The fire had almost burned out when they walked into the living room. CT added some kindling wood and a log, and soon the fire cast flickering shadows on the opposite wall.

"Let's see this tree of yours," Emma said, teasing. CT got on his hands and knees, picked up the end of the string of lights and turned to plug it into the socket, then paused.

"Oh, Sheez, Look!" he said and showed her the wrong end of the string of lights.

Emma burst into laughter.

"Ah, but I've surprised you," he said as he plugged in another string of lights and the entire tree lit up.

"Oh, it's lovely," she said. "And you certainly fooled me."

They sat side by side on the sofa facing the fire. CT picked up the Bible to read the Christmas story in Luke.

"And it came to pass in those days, that there went out a decree from Caesar Augustus, that all the world should be taxed . . .," CT began. He read even beyond the story of the first Christmas night and into the account of the family's going to the temple for Jesus' naming, all in chapter two of Luke. Finally realizing that he had gone beyond the account of that night, he stopped somewhat awkwardly.

72

"I have a surprise for you," Emma said. She opened the book containing "'Twas the Night Before Christmas," which she had hidden beside the sofa. Emma spoke with childlike awe of the mythical Santa Claus, a right jolly old elf, bringing toys to children throughout the world using a sleigh pulled by eight tiny reindeer. They sat on the sofa, close to each other, and let the fire die out.

Later holiday seasons added some slight changes to their planned celebrations. They combined Thanksgiving dinners with Aunt Mary and Uncle Brigham and their children, alternating hosting. Emma's father occasionally traveled from Cedar Valley to join them, at least for Thanksgiving. Some things remained the same: Emma and CT continued to have Christmas Eve together, alone in their home.

10
"Reunion"

One hot September night just after
Mr. Reynolds returned to live in his home
on Harvard Street in Salt Lake City, CT
was not catching the Interurban back to
the station west of Draper. He had told
Emma the night before that he'd be
working late and would stay over at the
Peery Hotel. About seven thirty that night
he turned off the light over his desk and
left Frank and Pearsall, Accountants, to
find some supper; he knew he really
wanted something more than a bite to eat.
He walked the short distance north to
Second South and looked east on the
north side of the street to towards
Victor's. He crossed Second South and
turned east, hoping. Pausing at the top of
the steps to Victor's, he glanced around
wondering if anyone was watching him.
Of course, he saw no one watching him.
After entering Victor's, he stopped to
adjust his eyes to the darker interior.

"CT!" a voice behind him spoke. Anyone watching closely could have seen his shoulders and neck stiffen, tighten briefly. CT felt goose pimples surge over his arms. He relaxed and turned around to face Roger.

"I hoped I would see you here," he said, smiling. "What are you drinking?"

"Thanks, a beer. But we have to sit down over there in one of the booths. It is, after all, a cafe."

"What's the special tonight?" CT asked the waitress when she came to the booth. "I'll have one of those," pointing to Roger's beer, "and bring him another. And two specials."

"Well, how's life treating you?" Roger asked. "I haven't seen you since the wedding. I began to wonder if you'd been converted."

"No, that's not happening. I don't know. It's. . . Let's not talk about that. I'm taking a break tonight from all that, working late, staying over at the Peery. What are you doing with yourself?"

"Still coaching swimming at Deseret. I also swim with an adult team, though we don't have a lot of competition from other teams. Ogden has a couple of adult teams, divided into varsity and adults. And of course, the YMCA fields a team and so does the 'U' and Weber College. But that's the extent of our competition."

"Have you been teaching any other University men how to swim?" CT asked, smiling.

"No. University men know how to swim. Well, all except one . . ." Roger looked at CT, his eyes sparkling. "And he knows how to swim now. How long's it been since you last went swimming?"

"I haven't seen a swimming pool since I passed the test. No, wait . . . you and me went swimming once about two years ago just before I got married."

76

"No, that was during the summer after you graduated. That was the last time. You're gonna forget how. You might even sink like lead."

"You promised I had enough air in me I wouldn't sink."

"Perhaps I was full of hot air."

"Well, you floated."

"Yes, even you did," Roger reminded him.

"Man, it's so good to see you. I've been starving for your company."

"That's why we need to go swimming. After we eat, let's go for a ride, then over to Deseret Gym. We'll do as we did when I taught you."

After eating, CT and Roger walked to the back entrance of Victor's and out into the alley connection to Regent Street. Roger put his arm around CT's neck and squeezed his shoulder.

They noticed two men watching them. One was sitting on a stoop, facing the other man. No one said anything. When Roger and CT had passed the two men, Roger asked, "Do you know James? Do you know what they're doing?"

"No," CT said, then paused, thinking.

After reaching Roger's parked car on Regent Street, Roger removed his arm from around CT's shoulders. "Climb in," he said. As they drove away, CT put his arm around Roger's shoulders.

City Creek flows out of the mountains just north of downtown Salt Lake City, running between Capitol Hill on the west and the hill to the east where the Avenues section of the city was built. The street leading along the stream into the canyon ran through a couple of small blocks of houses just north of North Temple. After passing the houses along City Creek, they drove into Memory Grove, still being prepared as a memorial to the soldiers who died in the War. Roger continued driving up the canyon into the woods above Memory Grove. The road above Memory Grove was dirt and narrow. A quarter of a mile beyond Memory Grove, Roger turned the car around so it faced down canyon, turned off the headlights, and then the motor.

CT turned to Roger. "It's been too long since I've spent some time with you. I've missed you."

"I've missed you, too" Roger responded. "Tell me what it's like to live in Draper."

"Well, I have chores to do morning and night. We have a dozen hens and a rooster. Each morning and evening, I need to check that their water is running through the trough and draining outside the coop, not flooding onto the floor. I feed them scratch, a mixture of wheat and corn, and laying mash. Also at night, I gather the eggs they've laid.

During the summers we have a steer, a yearling beef calf that we fatten to be slaughtered each fall for meat in our locker we rent at the meat company. As a wedding present, Emma's father gave us three ewes and a ram, and last year all the ewes lambed; we fatten the lambs during the summer to put more meat in our locker. I feed them some hay and grain each night—well hay only in the winter—and let them out into the pasture with the calf for the day. It makes for long days, since I have to catch the Interurban by seven fifteen each morning. The station is about five miles away in Riverton.

"Until the first of this month, my father was living with us and I'd ride with him to the station. Now that he's moved back to the city, Emma drives me down to the station. I usually return to Draper by 7:00 every evening, which means doing the farm chores in the dark in the winter. It's okay, but I'm a city boy. I miss getting together with the boys on weekend nights, playing poker, going to ball games and parties.

"I've wondered about my frat brothers. I don't hear from them and don't even know if they still live here." After a long pause, CT continued, "That life is over and gone. I miss it."

Roger started the car and began the drive back down to the city. "You don't have to be so isolated, CT. You can always stay in town more often."

CT remained silent, then Roger continued, "Are you ready for a swim?"

"Yes," CT answered.

11
"Swimming Again"

Driving out of City Creek Canyon that September night, Roger and CT went west along North Temple and easily found a parking place. They crossed North Temple and walked through LDS University campus, in which Deseret Gym functioned as the high school gym as well as a gymnasium for the adults in the downtown area.

The gym was nearing closing time, so Roger didn't need his keys to gain access; they just walked in. At the dressing room door, the attendant said hello as they walked in, knowing Roger as staff. They killed some time, chatting in the dressing room, then as most men still there finally left, Roger retrieved swimsuits from the storeroom and began changing. CT undressed slowly, taking special care to place his shirt and tie in the locker and hang his slacks carefully hung by a belt loop. Soon Roger was waiting, holding a towel for each of them, and watching CT, still naked.

"You'll do okay," he said. "I know it's been quite some time. You may be thinking you've forgotten everything. It'll come back quickly."

CT looked up at him and smiled. "You're right. I'm sure I've forgotten almost everything."

"Just remember one thing. You will not sink, you'll float. There's too much air in your lungs for you to sink. Let's go."

Roger headed out into the pool room. CT picked up the swimsuit Roger had placed on the bench and pulled it on. He walked to the door. The pool was empty; the room only partially lit by two lights still turned on. Roger had walked to the deep end by the time CT came from the dressing room. Roger, watching for CT's entrance, timed his smooth, water-slicing dive so CT would see it. He swam under the surface to the shallow end with

83

CT admiring the lithe swimmer. He surfaced and swung one arm onto the surface, spraying CT with water.

"Come on in. Let's review what you learned."

CT shivered slightly as he walked down the steps into the pool. It was cold, but not quite as cold as the spray Roger had just sent to him.

"Show me how you do the backstroke," Roger said.

CT lay back into the water and swung his right arm up over his head. As he brought it back through the water, he swung his left arm up and over his head. Roger swam beside CT, watching closely. When CT touched the pool wall, he turned around, and they swam back to the shallow end. This time, CT's arm hit the wall before he realized he had arrived. Abruptly he stood up, shocked, realizing that he might have hit the wall with his head.

"Yes, you need to be careful while swimming the back stroke—try to be aware when you near the wall. While we're here, put your hands against the wall and show me how you breathe doing the crawl."

CT practiced the breathing, holding onto the wall, but when they turned away from the wall and started to swim to the other side, CT's old fear resurged. He kept his face out of the water and inhaled all the air he possibly could and blew it all out before gasping to fill his lungs again.

"Whoa, whoa, whoa!" Roger called out. "Watch." He set off to catch up with CT, placing his face under water, then turning his face out of the water as his right arm passed above his head, and gently inhaled. He turned his head back into the water and exhaled as he brought his right arm down through the water. After four strokes, he stopped. "You don't need so much air. Gasping just exhausts you; you'll hyperventilate."

After a few minutes of review work, Roger suddenly surface dove, grabbed CT's leg, and standing up, turned CT upside down. Sputtering, CT came up and the wrestling match was on.

Finally, Roger paused. Looking CT in the eyes, "You're okay," he said, hugging CT. "See, there's nothing to be afraid of. Stay aware of what's going on, but you can swim and have a good time. It's so good to see you." They stood holding each other, staring into each other's eyes.

"I guess we'd better get you to your hotel. You need some sleep before work tomorrow."

They showered, dressed, and Roger made sure that everything at the gym was locked properly before they walked to his car. Roger drove to the Peery Hotel, and parked in an empty spot just west of the front entrance of the hotel.

"It's been so good to be together tonight," Roger said, turning off the ignition of the car.

"God, it sure has been. I've missed the city. I've missed you!"

"We need to do this much more often, CT," Roger said.

CT sat, suddenly quiet. He realized how much he agreed with Roger, how much he wanted to be with him, yet how impossible it all was. He couldn't stay over weekends; staying frequently on any night could so easily rouse suspicion in Emma, and anyone could casually say something that would get to his father. *Could I live a double life?* CT wondered.

"I'm scared. I can't stay in town very often. What would happen if. . . if Emma. . .?" CT said.

Roger reached his arm over and squeezed CT's shoulder. They hugged again. "I really would like to see you more."

"I'll see what I can do," CT said.

They continued hugging, and Roger kissed him. CT felt the tingle run down his spine. Then he climbed out of the car.

"Good night," he said through the open window. "Take care of yourself." He watched as Roger drove west on Third South, then turned and entered the hotel. When he reached his room on the third floor, he went to the window. Below the street was empty.

CT sobbed.

12
"Return to Nowhere"

Four long months after CT went to Victor's and saw Roger, he finally was able to plan another escape to the city. The holidays were over; it was still too early for lambing season. He decided on a Thursday night, primarily because he couldn't miss doing the weekend chores on a Saturday morning, so Friday night was out. On Monday morning that week, just as he got out of the car at the Interurban station, he said to Emma, "Oh, I'm going to have to work late on Thursday, so I'll get a room at the Peery."

"Oh," she responded quietly.

That afternoon during the drive from the station to their house, she asked, "Why do they need you to stay late?"

"Well, I guess they figure that we won't get the contracts done in time if we don't put in extra time."

"Contracts?"

"Yes, we do accounting and auditing for companies that need reports quarterly, sometimes even monthly, throughout the year."

"It seems strange that you don't have to stay. . ." and she stopped.

CT waited in the silence, wondering if he should ask what she wanted to say or just let it drop.

"Was there a reason for Thursday night?"

"I just chose Thursday 'cause if I stayed Friday night, I wouldn't be home for Saturday morning work around the place."

"Well, that makes sense."

Sometime later, Emma asked, "Can't they find someone in the office who doesn't have to catch the Interurban to get home? It seems a shame you should have to stay late when you have no way home after 6:45. Streetcars in the city run much later than that."

"They probably haven't asked anyone. I'm actually volunteering to do this because the work needs to be done soon, and I'm afraid I won't get it done in time without extra work."

"You're volunteering? They haven't asked you to stay late?"

"Yes," he answered. "I guess I should have asked you first. Will it interfere with any of your plans?"

"No. But. . ."

"I don't do it often," CT countered.

Emma stopped asking and did not bring the subject up on Tuesday or Wednesday. CT relaxed. Wednesday night, CT spoke aloud to himself as he gathered the eggs and fed the animals.

"Finally, it's Thursday! Thursday! I thought it would never come. I can't wait to see Roger again."

Thursday the clock inched backwards. *My God,* he thought, glancing at the offending clock. *It was ten o'clock an hour ago; it's only quarter past now.*

At 11:30, Mr. Pearsall watched him look again at the clock. "What's eating you, CT? You've looked at that damned clock half a dozen times this morning."

"Oh. I don't know. Nothing really. I guess the day just seems to be going slow."

He glanced over at Mr. Pearsall, then returned his eyes to the work on his desk.

Finally, other workers started pulling out the final sheet and carbon copies from their typewriters, covering the machines, cleaning up their desks, finishing their day's work. CT kept his

92

calculating machine on, working on a report, grateful that the others were leaving.

"You going to work all night?" Mr. Pearsall asked.

"Oh no," CT answered. "I'm staying a little late to get the figures for the Anderson report done. But it's not a problem."

"Okay. But don't stay so late you can't get home."

"I've got a room for the night at the Peery. I'll be fine. Thanks." *Oh, no. What if Mr. Pearsall sees my father and tells him that I'm staying in the city?*

At 8:00 o'clock, CT turned off the light over his desk in Frank and Pearsall, Accountants. He quickly left the office, checking that the door was locked, left the building and turned right on Main Street, walking north to Second South. *What if Roger isn't at Victor's? I should have called him earlier in the week. Maybe he's out of town at a swim meet.*

After crossing Second South, he turned right toward Victor's, slowing down as he approached the stairs going down to the door. *Well, even if he's not here, I need something to eat,* he thought and resumed his pace.

Once inside he scanned the room but did not see Roger. He walked to an empty booth and sat down.

"What can I get you?" the girl in a short skirt and apron asked.

"What's on the menu tonight?" he asked.

"We have hot beef sandwich or hot turkey sandwich. Both have mashed potatoes an' gravy and canned green beans. Or there's meatloaf."

"I'll take the hot beef sandwich. Do you have beer? Uh.... No, I'll take a coke."

94

"Sure thing," she said. turning away.

CT looked around the room again. He couldn't see all the occupants of the other booths from his seat, but he could easily see that Roger was not sitting at the counter. "Damn," he muttered. "I should have tried to get in touch with him."

He got up to go to the restroom so he could look at the people sitting in other booths, still hoping. In the restroom, he noted that one of the stalls was occupied and wondered if perhaps Roger might be there. After dallying a couple of minutes to see if the man would come out of the stall, he returned to his booth, looking at the people in the booths he had not seen on his way to the restroom. "Damn," he repeated.

After sitting down in his booth, he kept looking at the restroom door, hoping to see the man come out. When he came out, CT saw he was in his fifties, maybe even sixties. Obviously not Roger.

He ate his dinner slowly, hoping Roger might come in. Finally finishing his meal, he picked up the check the waitress had left when she brought his food. Standing up, he fished out sixty cents for a tip and walked toward the cash register. Then he saw the bartender and turned to him.

"Hi, you know Roger, don't you?" he asked.

"Sure, I remember him."

"Does he come in anymore?"

"Uh, where you been? Roger left for San Francisco about two, three months ago. He had this student at LDS who was really good at swimming. Roger suggested they go to Berkeley, as he knew the swimming coach at the University, and he thought if the coach there could see the kid during his final year of high school, the kid would have a good chance of getting a scholarship. Roger got a job teaching swimming at a gym."

"Does he. . . Do you know his address? I'd like to write him, keep in touch."

"Haven't heard from him for a while. Don't have his address any more."

"If he writes again, please save his address for me. I work at Frank and Pearsall's and come in fairly often at lunch time."

"Sure thing."

CT paid his bill and left Victor's, slowly climbing the steps to the street. *Now what?* The city held no attraction now. *I wouldn't know any of the men living at the Phi Delt house; I've been gone over five years. To them I'm an old man.*

Without thinking, he walked north along Main Street past South Temple, and entered the grounds of LDS University, where he'd gone to high school. The main campus buildings stood on the outside of the road from Main Street that looped to

97

the right into the middle of the block on an elongated circle; no potent memories remained. Just beyond the easternmost of the campus buildings on The Circle stood Deseret Gym, where the high school teams played basketball and held phys-ed classes, and the community had access to all facilities. As he approached the gym, he thought of going swimming, but realized it would be closed by this time. *Besides, Roger won't be there.*

He paused at the entrance to the gym, then walked on to South Temple. He wandered on east to State Street and then south. The seedier businesses along State Street, shuttered at this hour of night, further desolated him. When he reached 300 South St., he turned west for the two blocks to the Peery. There he rented a room for the night and climbed the stairs to the third floor, unlocked and entered his room. He went to the window which looked out on the street. Below, the street was empty.

A month later, as CT entered the offices of Frank & Pearsall, Accountants,

98

he saw the morning edition of the *Salt Lake Tribune* lying on a table by the door. A headline immediately caught his attention, "Salt Lake Man Killed in California Car Crash."

No, no. Oh, God, no. Prescient of the contents, he picked up the paper and pulled it to his chest, hiding the article's title from anyone. *I can't read this at my desk; everyone will see me. Where can I possibly go to read this?*

He walked to the door from the front reception area into the workroom containing the workers' desks. He left his lunch on his desk as he walked by to go to the rear hall connecting the workroom with the breakroom, the restrooms, and the stairwell connecting all the floors with a ground floor exit.

Others will be in the breakroom drinking coffee; I can't go there. I'm not going to read it in the men's restroom. Ah, the stairwell.

CT entered the stairwell, climbed three steps, and sat down. He brought the newspaper down from his chest to his lap and began reading. The crash occurred on the coast highway south of San Francisco on a foggy night. The car careened into the guardrail, bounced over it, and fell to the rocks and ocean below.

Although CT read the rest of the article about Roger's career coaching high school swimming at LDS, swimming on the AAU and the University teams, and his surviving parents and siblings, CT fathomed none of it.

I can't go to his funeral service. I don't know any of his family. They probably wouldn't want me if they knew. I can't say anything. Not to anyone.

Numbness enveloped him. Everything turned to grey. For two days he remembered nothing of work; whatever he did, he did automatically and remembered none of it.

100

He kept the newspaper, sequestered in his desk. He didn't dare take it home.

For weeks, he refused to go to Victor's. *The bartender—or anyone else—may remember seeing us together and say something. I can't take anyone saying he's sorry. I'd probably bawl. And what if no one remembers us? What if no one says anything about Roger? No, I cannot go there.*

13

"Dreams"

A couple of years earlier, on an evening in mid-October, as CT drove the car into the driveway, he saw the meat packing crew working in the corral. Tied by its hind quarters from the crossbeam, one of the lambs stretched down, skinned, the outer layer of its fat gleaming white. He turned his face away; yet he felt a tightening in his stomach. He quickly climbed the steps to the back porch and entered the kitchen.

Weeks later, when he was coming down with a bad cold, he dreamed he was entering the driveway, and the lamb was hanging from the crossbeam. He saw red oozing down from the lamb's crotch across the white fat covering its flesh. Remembering he had cut out the lamb's testicles, shuddering with guilt, he walked toward the corral. *Maybe I can take the body down.* Then he realized that it was

102

not a lamb, but a man, hanging upside
down, still bleeding slowly from his
crotch. CT couldn't see the man's face.
Who is it? Who hanged him there? And
the dream ended.

Occasionally, the dream recurred.
Not often, not regularly. Each time, CT
awoke, agonized over its meaning. *Who is
the man? How did he get there? Why is he
there? Why can't I help him?*

Several days after learning of the
accident on the Pacific Coast Highway
south of San Francisco, he saw in his
dream that the man hanging from the
crossbeam and bleeding from his crotch
was Roger. Weeping, he approached the
body and tried to take it down; suddenly
he was awake. He shuddered. He tried
rolling over but dreaded falling asleep,
being in that dream again. He needed
sleep, but fearing the dream, slept only
fitfully. Two hours later, he gave up,
arose and began preparing to go into
work.

The next night, exhausted from his farmer's chores, from accounting work, and lack of sleep, he fell into a deep sleep, waking only once and quickly falling back to sleep. He was still tired the next morning but grateful that the dream had not haunted him again. As the days went by without a recurrence of the dream, he finally put it out of his mind.

Later that winter, he caught a cold that threatened the quality of his sleep and left him tired throughout each day. The second night of his cold, the dream came back. Now, he knew immediately that the carcass hanging with its legs spread eagle was Roger and that he was helpless to rescue him. He could not find the ropes from the pulley attached to the crossbeam that would allow him to lower Roger's body. He finally embraced the body and wept. Then he awoke.

Afterwards, whenever he felt slightly ill, a cold coming on, or especially something more serious, he dreaded the return of the dream. It did return, at least once, each time he was ill.

Finally, one night in the dream he managed to get the body into his arms, though he did not see how the ropes came loose from the crossbeam. As he accepted the body being lowered into his arms, he realized that the man standing there accepting the body was Roger. Roger lowered the lamb from the crossbeam then sat on the ground holding the emasculated lamb—CT—stretched across his lap, pale and dead. Roger wept.

CT awoke, somber.

14
"Emma, CT, and Sarah"

CT brought home his paycheck each Friday night and gave it to Emma to deposit in their checking account at the bank in Sandy. She had the checkbook to pay for groceries, drug store items, her appointments at the beauty parlor, and the usual bills that came via mail.

During the first month of their marriage, they did not have a checking account. One day she had asked for money to have her hair done, and CT gave her a twenty-dollar bill. When she returned, he asked, "Where's the change?"

"There isn't any change. There never will be any change."

CT saw the light. Shortly thereafter, he decided they should have a joint checking account. He told her of his decision one Saturday and then came home early from Frank and Pearsall, Accountants, on the following Monday. They went together to the bank in Sandy to set up the joint account, one for which either signature was sufficient.

Checkbooks in those days were large ledgers, with three or four checks per page and each check had a stub at the binding on which one could write the payee, the amount of the check, and the balance in the account going forward. He handed Emma the checkbook and never questioned her expenditures.

Every month, CT balanced the checkbook against the statement mailed from the bank.

"Honey," he began one night while balancing the checkbook. "You haven't written anything in the check stubs for check numbers 109 and 110, yet the checks aren't here. Have you issued either or both these checks? If so, to who and for how much?"

"Check numbers 109 and 110?" she asked. "I don't know. I went to Uncle Miller's the other day and I guess I issued one of those checks to him. I don't remember for how much."

"Honey, you have to record on the stub who you pay and how much."

"Yes, I know I should do this. But I have to take checks with me on errands. It's not like I have the stub with me when I write a check while I'm out shopping. By the time I return home, I sometimes don't remember to write in the checkbook."

"Well, you have to do that. I can't balance the checkbook if I can't find out how much you spent."

This conversation was not a one-time event; Emma made the same mistake several times over the years. When smaller check books finally came out with duplicate sheets, she automatically made a copy as she wrote the check. Occasionally, however, she made the mistake of tearing out both the check and its copy sheet.

Emma appreciated CT's trust when it came to finances, but from early in their marriage, she wondered about his lack of passion toward her. It wasn't that CT didn't spend time with her. They slept in the same bed every night; they ate their breakfasts and evening suppers together, often enjoying conversations about politics, current events, happenings in the town. They read together, usually on Sunday afternoons.

But they didn't play together. He never took her dancing, even to the occasional dances sponsored by their ward. Rarely, they would cuddle, sitting together on the living room sofa. He was kind and sensitive but sometimes, from her point of view, in odd ways.

He blanched when it came time to slaughter the lambs, always insisting that they have the slaughterhouse crew do it entirely, even when the crew did it at their farm. He didn't willingly kill and dress a chicken for dinner.

Is he involved with another woman? she wondered. For three or four years after they married, he had occasionally stayed overnight in the city. *Do I ask him if he has another woman?* She finally approached Aunt Mary.

"Aunt Mary, how often. . .? Uh, CT doesn't seem . . . He doesn't seem to want . . . sex with me very often. Should I worry about this? What is normal for a young couple? Do you mind if I ask you these questions?"

Aunt Mary hesitated a bit. "No, I don't mind your asking. I hesitate only because I don't know what to say. Brigham doesn't initiate sex very often; sometimes I do. When we do have sex, he seems to enjoy it, and he works to have me enjoy it as well. What seems to be bothering you? If I may ask."

"Well, I don't seem to know what to say either. We hardly ever have sex.

110

He's kind, gentle, and considerate of me, and.... But I don't think he enjoys sex with me. Do you think he might have another woman somewhere? Oh, that's a terrible thing to say!"

"No, no," Aunt Mary quickly answered. "You're concerned so we should talk about it. I'll watch more closely, but I haven't seen anything to suggest he has another woman, at least not here in Draper. I'm sure most women in the ward would try to hide any gossip from both you and me, but I can't imagine that someone wouldn't slip up and say something in my presence or yours."

"Oh, I've not heard any gossip about CT and me. I'd be mortified if such word got out!"

"Yes, I'm sure you would." After pausing, Aunt Mary continued, "There're a few busybodies in the ward; if anyone had such an idea, we'd hear about it. So, I sincerely doubt he has another woman here or in Sandy or Crescent. Talk would have come out before this long."

111

"He stayed overnight in the city occasionally in these past few years. I wonder. . . Should I ask him?"

"Oh, I don't know. I don't know how to advise you there. Once you've said something, you can't take it back. You may never know how much asking that question may hurt him and you. Let me think about this a few days."

"Please don't say anything to anybody, including Uncle Brigham. I can't abide that this doubt would get out to anyone else."

"I will obey your restriction. I understand. Although I would have asked Brig, but you said not to, so I'll keep this to myself."

Neither woman brought up the subject in the next couple of days, and the longer they waited, the more comfortable silence became and the more hesitant each felt to broach the subject.

Eventually, Emma did allude to the distance between herself and CT when she asked, "Could I have caused his coolness because I'm too heavy or I don't make myself beautiful for him before he comes home from work? Do I not keep a clean enough house for him?"

"You're not too heavy, you're beautiful, and you keep a clean house. That can't be a cause," Aunt Mary responded.

Then CT spent another night in Salt Lake City. Still unsure of her status but becoming daring, upon his return the following evening, she asked, "Did you stay with Sarah?"

"Sarah? Who's Sarah?"

"Well, I don't know that her name is Sarah, only that you stay in the City, I suppose to see someone."

CT paused and, relieved that Emma apparently didn't know about Roger, chuckling, said, "Oh sure. I visited

113

Sarah between leaving Frank and
Pearsall's at 8:15 and checking into the
Peery at 8:35. She isn't very hospitable."

Eventually, Emma realized that if
he were unfaithful during those overnight
stays, the episodes were not an affair so
much as perhaps visits to a prostitute; he
didn't stay often enough for there to be an
affair. She hoped he wasn't seeing
prostitutes. After talking with Aunt Mary,
she also realized Draper was so small she
would have heard gossip if there had been
another woman in Draper or any of the
neighboring towns.

Eventually, Emma began teasing
CT about "Sarah" whenever he came
home late. One night, she forgot to meet
him at the Interurban stop. When she
finally arrived at the station to pick him
up, she wryly said, "Well I felt I should
give you some time to visit Sarah."

"Doggone, you should've told me
this morning that I'd have time. I didn't
know to tell her to meet me."

"Well, you know how the first wife often cheats the newer wives of their time with the man. You'll just have to adjust. I'm sure Sarah will survive."

"But will I?" he asked.

"Yes, you will also."

After he lost his job with Frank and Pearsall, he worked in Draper, coming home after work every night. They spent Saturdays working at home—she finishing housework and he cleaning the animal pens or repairing things—and Sundays at church, and reading between dinner and evening sacrament meeting. There was no time for him to visit Sarah. Emma realized he was faithful, even if essentially platonic with her.

15
"October, 1933"

The row of poplar trees extending west from the road running in front of CT and Emma's house stood as a wind break, dividing fields. The browning leaves of the poplars took on a glow from the October afternoon light. In the pasture north of the poplars, the grass and alfalfa had recovered enough from the last hay mowing a month earlier that numerous new green alfalfa leaves glittered in the light. South of the poplars, the corn stalks reflected the light in soft dun.

Emma sat at the writing desk before the west window in the living room of their home staring out the window and beyond the fields. She saw none of the beauty. On a sheet of stationery, she had begun, "October 25th, 1933" and below after a blank line, "Dear Daddy."

"Dear Daddy, Maryelle is thriving. Everyone here is well and fine," she wrote. She intended to continue with chat about Aunt Mary and Uncle Brigham, about recent news of other families her father knew, about CT and their life together. She would ask about all the family and neighbors scattered throughout the valley. She had wanted to write such a letter, but she could not.

Whatever I write, I'm afraid I'll sound like I'm complaining. Maybe I would be, she thought. *If I'm not careful, Daddy will think CT is not good to us, and that isn't so. He's so considerate and kind. He doesn't anger, and I do. I explode, and he's so calm. Even when he brought home the letter from Frank and Pearsall terminating him and containing his final pay check.*

"We are very happy with CT's work," they had written. "We would be happy to have continued employing him, but business has dropped off so dramatically, we have had to terminate several employees."

She also realized she must not seem ungrateful of Aunt Mary and Uncle Brigham. They continued to help supplement what Emma and CT and now Mary Louise needed, even after CT got work at the feed store as a laborer in the warehouse.

So, her letter sat on the writing table, with a date, a salutation, and barely a sentence. *If I just write the pleasantries, he'll know something's wrong. I can't hide it in trivia.* She picked up the pen, put its cap on it, opened the drawer of the writing table and stored the pen and the sheet of paper within. Then hearing the baby fussing, she walked out of the living room and up the stairs to the baby's room.

"There, there," she cooed to Mary Louise. "It's time to get you up, change your daidie, and get some supper." Laying the baby down on a table, she continued talking to her, sang a couple of ditties, and tickled her tummy and her feet as she cleaned her and wrapped her in a clean diaper. "There. All ready to help with

118

supper," Emma said, picking Mary Louise up to carry her downstairs.

As they descended, Emma heard CT coming through the back door into the kitchen. "My goodness," she cried out, "I'm late getting supper. I'm sorry."

"No problem. I'm home a little early tonight," CT responded as Emma hurried into the kitchen. "Ah, let me take Maryelle while you fix supper."

CT took Emma into a hug and kissed her forehead. Then he took Mary Louise from her, raised her high above his head. Up high, he wiggled her around, then suddenly brought her down as if in a free fall to his chest. She squealed. He lifted her back up and she squealed again, anticipating her fall back to his chest. Down again with Mary Louise squealing. Up, then down, more squeals; up, then down. CT sat down on one of the kitchen chairs and played pony riding, crossing his legs and balancing Mary Louise on his foot, moving her up and down slowly for

119

the walk, bouncing for a trot, and racing
for the gallop, then suddenly slowly again.

I wish he'd play . . . Emma
thought, then dismissed it quickly out of
her mind. But as CT played with the baby,
the thought returned. *I wish he had as
much fun with me as he does with the
baby. Now quit being ungrateful!* she
remonstrated herself.

16
"Mary, Mentor"

Emma first took Mary Louise to Church when she was just two months old. In the meantime, Aunt Mary had visited Emma and the baby several times. "Oh, sweet Maryelle," Aunt Mary cooed as she held the smiling baby. Maryelle smiled in response to this loving woman. She probably sensed that Aunt Mary and her mother loved each other deeply and she was safe in Aunt Mary's arms.

Aunt Mary's children usually came with her. After they had each held Maryelle at the beginning of their visits, they would then go outside to play, leaving Aunt Mary and Emma to talk and do household chores.

"Do you need any shopping?" Aunt Mary asked one Saturday.

"Yes, we do need some things. Can we go together?"

"Sure. I'll stay in the car with Maryelle while you shop for what you need. I don't think we should take her inside with a lot of other people yet."

"I'm sure you're right. Crowds mean a lot of bugs going around, and I don't want her to get sick. Thanks for the offer."

"Emma and I are going shopping to Uncle Miller's. We're taking the baby with us," Aunt Mary said to the children. "We'll be back in about a half hour. I'll buy some cookies for us all to share if you behave."

They got into CT and Emma's car and started off to the center of Draper and Uncle Miller's general store, where he sold various necessities in addition to groceries.

"You haven't baked bread for some time, have you?" Aunt Mary asked.

"No. I haven't. It takes so much strength to knead the bread enough and I just haven't felt up to it for a couple of months."

"Well, we can bake some this afternoon, so don't buy any bread. I can knead the dough if you can't. Do you have all the ingredients you'll need? Yeast, flour, sugar?"

"Yes, I've got flour on my list and some fresh vegetables if he's got any. We have sugar, spices, yeast, everything else we need for bread. I really appreciate your helping me with the bread. Oh, what kind of cookies did you want for the children?"

"Oh, yes. . . some oatmeal cookies with raisins, if he's got any."

After returning from shopping, Aunt Mary and Emma fixed sandwiches of roast pork and a fresh salad.

"Come to lunch," Aunt Mary called to the children from the kitchen door. "After you finish the salad and sandwich you can have a couple of cookies each."

"What kind did you get?" Jason, the older, asked.

"Oatmeal and raisin."

"Not chocolate chip? Gee whiz, why raisins?"

"Well, for one thing, they're good for you."

"Yeah, but dessert isn't supposed to be 'good for you.'"

"Well, oatmeal with raisins are the cookies we have. If you don't want any dessert, you don't have to have it."

After the children finished their lunch, Aunt Mary and Emma quickly washed the dishes and got ready to bake bread, chatting as they worked.

After kneading the dough a second time, then forming the loaves and setting them in pans to rise again before baking, they took a break.

124

"I'm whipped," Emma confessed. "And I only helped with the first kneading. You did half of that first kneading and almost all the second one. How do you get the energy?"

"Well, you have to keep at it. I'll continue to help, but you'll only gain stamina by pushing yourself to do more again and again."

Sometimes I think Reuben spoiled this young woman by hiring a cook to take care of all that responsibility, Aunt Mary thought. *Emma didn't pick up much in that line of work.*

Emma thought, *She's more like a mother to me than a slightly older friend. She expects me to work harder. She has a point; work is necessary to regain strength, but it sure isn't easy.*

The following Saturday, Aunt Mary had Emma bring Maryelle to her home.

"We're going to bake a batch of bread but cut the recipe in half. You're going to knead the dough. I'll help if you need me to."

Emma kneaded the dough. While it made her a little winded, doing only three loaves instead of the full batch made it decidedly easier.

"I'm a bit winded," she said after the first kneading. "But doing half a batch helped a lot."

She formed the dough into a ball and placed it in a bowl for the first rising.

After the bread had risen, Emma did the second kneading by herself. They divided the dough into three loaves and placed it in three pans to rise again before baking.

A week later, Aunt Mary and Emma baked bread again. Although this time, they baked a full batch, Emma did the first kneading entirely.

126

"You're doing very well," Aunt
Mary said.

"I don't feel weak at all," Emma
said. "You're right about working to gain
strength. Come to think of it, carrying
Maryelle around hasn't tired me as much
lately."

After Emma did the second
kneading, they cut the dough into six
portions, formed the loaves and placed
them into the pans to rise. They cleaned
up the dishes and kitchen while the bread
baked.

Aunt Mary went to the door to the
back yard when the bread was done and
called the children. "The bread is ready.
Come, have a slice with butter and
honey."

Noisily, the children entered the
kitchen and sat at the table. Emma sliced
one of the loaves and buttered the slices
so everyone could have some. Aunt Mary
spread the honey on the pieces for the
children to prevent a mess on the table.

"It's so good," Jason said after finishing his piece.

"Are you asking for more?" Aunt Mary asked smiling.

"Yes, please."

"Can I have another one too?" Sarah asked.

"Finish your first piece. Then we'll see," Aunt Mary said.

"It really is so good, fresh out of the oven with butter and honey," Emma said. "I think I could eat an entire loaf!"

"You and me both. But then what would we look like!"

"Yes, and neither of us can afford a whole new wardrobe," Emma said.

The first Sunday Emma took Mary Louise to church, all the sisters of the ward wanted to see the baby.

"Oh, my goodness," cooed one sister after another on seeing Maryelle.

Emma swelled with joy and pride.

"May I hold her?" Sister Fitzgerald requested, but when she took her, Mary Louise began to fuss. "Oh, dear," she responded. "I'd better give her back."

"Thank you," Emma half sighed, receiving the baby back. "Now, now, Maryelle," she cooed and rocked her gently.

"Well, you finally have a sweet little one," said Sister Smith. "Did you intend to wait so long?"

"Thank you," Emma responded. "She is so sweet the wait was worth it."

"Of course, you do remember our responsibility to build up Zion."

"Yes, indeed, we will teach Maryelle the gospel in word and deed,"

129

Emma countered, stressing slightly the final word.

Later alone with Aunt Mary, Emma confessed, "I have problems with a few of the sisters. Today, Sister Smith snidely commented upon the delay CT and I have had before having Maryelle. It hurts."

"It's really none of their business whether you wait or why," Aunt Mary answered.

"You're right. But it still smarts to have any of them make us inferior to. . . "

"Their comments don't make you inferior. Their opinion should not matter to you."

"How do I get to the place where their opinions don't matter?"

"Know within your heart that you are a very good mother and wife. You are, you know. So, remember that. The number of babies you have doesn't make your worth. The quality of lives those babies lead will be far more important than how many you have. Look around. You know a couple in the ward who have ten or eleven, I scarcely can keep up, and they're all terrors. *That* isn't building Zion;" Aunt Mary's emphasis brought both to laughter.

17
"Maryelle"

At times, Emma felt jealous of
Maryelle; the child had such a hold on
CT. CT loved Maryelle, obvious to any
observer. Sometimes Emma
felt—knew— CT loved Maryelle more
than he loved her. When Maryelle was
little, each night after his work at the feed
store, CT played with her. He *played* with
her. As she grew, he listened to her talk of
the things she had done each day. He took
her with him as he did the evening chores,
asking her questions and listening to her
prattle of her day's activities.

When gathering eggs, he showed
her how to reach into the nest and remove
the eggs and place them carefully in the
basket to take to the kitchen. The first
time a hen didn't scramble out of the nest
when they approached, she was afraid to
put her hand into the nest. He warned her
that the hen might peck at her hand, but

she wouldn't really hurt her. So, she put
her hand under the hen.

"Oh," she exclaimed. "It's so
warm under her. Why?"

"Her body is hotter than the air, so
you feel the warmth from her body. If she
turns setting, she'll have a clutch of eggs,
and she'll stay on the nest almost all the
time and keep the eggs warm 'til they
hatch. After they hatch, she'll give the
chicks a warm, safe place under her
wings."

Later in the spring one of the hens
did turn setting. CT showed Maryelle the
hutch he had built for the hen with straw
for a nest. The hen sat quiet until CT
reached his hand into the hutch, and she
clucked angrily at him and fluffed up her
feathers. "See, she is protecting the eggs."

CT nailed slats over the entry to
the hutch, locking the hen in and
predators out. He placed a pint bottle
filled with water with a drinking lid on it,
turned lid down so that the hen would be

able to drink. He set some grain on the ground near the nest so she would have something to eat. "We'll feed her this way and check her water every day until after the chicks hatch. Then, when they are a couple of days old, we'll take the slats off the hutch so she can take the chicks around the yard during the day and return to the hutch at night."

When they hatched, he took Maryelle to see them. "Oh!" she cried. "They're so cute, Can I hold them?"

"If any come out through the slats, I'll pick one up for you to hold." When he picked one up, it peeped loudly, the hen squawked angrily. "Hold out your hand but don't squeeze the chick. You don't want to hurt him."

"Oh! She's so soft and fuzzy. I love them," she squealed. She opened her hands wide, allowing the chick to escape. It fled into the hutch and disappeared into its refuge under the hen's wing.

134

Maryelle talked to him while he milked the cow Emma's grandfather had given them as a wedding present. He showed her how the cow would eat rolled barley from her hand, gently picking up the grains with her upper lip and not biting Maryelle's hand. "It tickles." she cried.

"Yes, she's very gentle even though she's pretty big."

Emma couldn't help it. She felt a competition between her little daughter and herself for the love of CT. Maryelle filled most of CT's free hours, and Maryelle made him smile and laugh. But Emma was Maryelle's mother and also loved her. Emma showed Maryelle what she loved.

Emma loved to read. She learned that if she planned her days, she could have an hour or so in the early afternoons to read. Having freed up some time from household duties, she turned to the collection of books they had accumulated or to books checked out from the county library. After Maryelle was born, Emma read to her as part of her own reading time.

She had begun taking Maryelle to the county library in Midvale after her third birthday. Sometimes they would spend an hour in the library selecting books; two or three picture books for Maryelle and a novel or biography that Emma wanted to read. It became a habit. Every two weeks, they would return to the library. Because Emma would read aloud to Maryelle each afternoon just after nap time, Maryelle soon learned to read, and then together they would read aloud the books Maryelle selected.

18
"Epiphany, My Baby"

Emma had hoped that when the baby was born, when their family began to grow, CT would somehow really be there for her, that he would look on her with passionate love. After Maryelle was born, as Emma watched her beloved baby grow, watched the love between father and daughter swell, she still hoped CT would grow to love her. As the years passed without any change in CT's response to her, Emma grew to accept their situation.

Then, one late September afternoon in 1940, she walked into the living room of their home and saw the sunlight shining through the front window, over the surface of her writing table, and diagonally across the floor and onto the north wall opposite the fireplace. she turned and looked at the fireplace, a fireplace without a fire... *There is no fire. No hope of fire. There never will be fire.*

Two nights later, she begged CT. "I want another baby. I want a baby boy. Give me that. Please. Please," and after a short silence, "You owe me that."

He yielded.

Within three days, Emma knew that she had conceived another baby, and she knew that the baby was a boy. From that very beginning, she cradled him, singing lullabies as she held her hands over her womb. After the years of the lonely, worrying . . . wondering why, this was an awesome dawning. Morning sickness still invaded her days some weeks. As she gained weight and retained water and labored through the physical struggle, she rejoiced, singing, glowing.

Emma and CT agreed that the child would not be named Charles after CT, nor Thomas after Mr. Reynolds. CT suggested Reuben, after Emma's father. "He isn't a Reuben," Emma said pensively.

"Brigham," CT offered.

"I'd hesitate to name him after Uncle Brigham when we didn't name him after daddy. Perhaps we should go with a name not in either family."

"Well, Joseph was the prophet of the Lord."

"Samuel was also, really two Samuels. The one in the Old Testament and Samuel the Lamanite," Emma offered.

"Caleb," CT suddenly said. "I don't know why that name comes to me. I don't know who he was, I've only heard his name. Was he in the Book of Mormon or the Bible?"

"Caleb. Yes, I like that," Emma answered.

So, they named him after the one who brought good news to the camp of Israel, the one who lived long and received his inheritance. Like Caleb of

139

old, however, his good news for the whole camp of Israel, his coming, didn't alter anything.

After Caleb was born, Emma continued to cuddle him, hold him close, "Caleb, my baby, you sweetheart. You are my sweet little one. How I love you. I could eat you up." She would put her face into his tummy and growl while exhaling, tickling him. He would laugh.

When Caleb began to crawl, Emma got on her hands and knees and crawled with him, playing. "I'm gonna get you," she whispered, crawling closer, "I'm going to catch you. Here I come." He squealed and crawled faster. Then she would reach out her hand and, catching his foot, gently pull him to her, roll him over, and blow on his stomach, bringing on more laughter. Finally, she would pick him up, cradle him in her arms and sing him a lullaby. Emma recited poems and read stories to him at least once every day.

Emma relished being so close to Caleb, rejoiced unabashedly in her time with him. Shortly before Caleb turned three, however, she began to worry that CT was not bonding with him as easily as he had with Maryelle.

"You know," she said one evening to CT, "I think Caleb is old enough to go with you to do chores. At least some of them, feeding the chickens and gathering the eggs. I'm not sure about the cow yet."

"Yes, you're right. I'll take him with me. We'll do the chickens first. Then I'll bring him and the eggs in and go back to feed the sheep and cow and milk her. With spring here shortly, I expect we'll have a setter soon; he'll love the chicks just as Maryelle did."

Next evening when CT got ready to go do chores, Emma said to Caleb, "Why don't you go with Daddy and Maryelle to do chores?"

"'Kay," Caleb said and went with them.

"Oh, Mommy," Caleb squealed when they returned. "I getted 'n egg. Daddy held me up an' I getted it. The hen said 'pwahk, pwahk, pwahk' when we walked up to the nests."

"Did she fly out of the nest?"

"Yeah. She scare me. But Daddy said it was okay."

He's growing up so fast. It's good for him to go with CT. Oh I do love him. Oh, I love CT as well, but. . . It's not the same. I still wish CT'd be romantic with me. . . but I'm okay. I guess I don't miss that as much now. He doesn't feel that way, so. . . It's okay.

Emma still had several hours with Caleb during the days. She continued reading to him during the afternoons after he awoke from his nap. One day, Caleb asked, "How do you know the story in the book?"

"These are letters," she answered pointing to the letters on the page. "When

142

the letters come together, they form words to tell the story. Do you want to learn the letters? They each have names. We can use one of Maryelle's books, telling about each of the letters."

They spent five minutes of each reading time, saying the alphabet from Maryelle's old alphabet book. Then Emma would read aloud one of the fairy stories. Occasionally, she would ask Caleb, "Can you point out an *A* on this page?" When he succeeded, she might ask him, "Where's an *M?*" This way, Caleb soon learned the different letters. At the same time, Emma taught him the sounds the different letters make.

Though Emma's relationship with Caleb began to change when CT took him to do the evening chores, they were still close. Caleb's relationship with CT also changed, but not quite as Emma had envisioned it would. True, Caleb had the same interests in the farm animals as Maryelle had shown. Caleb, however, eventually had this work as regular chores. By age six, he was tending the

143

chickens and helping feed the steers and sheep; by ten he was cleaning the manure from the pens by himself. Before he turned twelve, Caleb had learned how to milk the cow. CT was not a farmer; he was delighted to turn these chores over to Caleb and have more free time at home. Caleb and CT no longer shared daily farm time.

Part II Promises

Drawing, located on web site for All Saints
Episcopal Church of Selingrove, Pennsylvania, as
of 22 September 2020; image no longer on web
site, Dec 2021.

145

1
"BYU, 1959"

Caleb had looked forward to attending BYU ever since the girl he was dating in the autumn of his senior year in high school cancelled their date to the Harvest Ball, set up two weeks earlier, on the Monday before the dance. From then on in his senior year, his social life consisted of football, basketball, and baseball games.

At BYU, he got a room in a dorm in Helaman Halls. Though Draper is only some thirty-five miles from Provo, his first trip back to Draper that autumn was the day before Thanksgiving.

Since Emma knew Caleb loved history, she encouraged him to take other general education courses required for graduation before he took history. He listened.

146

He studied bacteriology fall quarter, liking the lectures and the reading, loving the lab section. The woman graduate assistant teaching the lab clearly loved her work, so everyone enjoyed the lab. One lab assignment was to bring a urine sample to examine under a microscope; everyone supposed they had all brought their own urine. The session was going along smoothly when one of the single women students called out, "What is this?!"

The lab assistant went to her microscope and looked. "Oh, that's spermatozoa—male sperm."

"What? Uh . . . But . . . . This isn't. . ." the student stammered, blushing.

Suddenly another woman in the lab rescued her. "Oh, Jenny forgot her sample, so I gave her part of mine. I guess you know what my husband and I did last night!" She blushed, and everyone laughed.

The lab assistant appreciated humor. . . and used it to teach more than lab techniques. Prior to Thanksgiving, she had the students examine samples of Salmonella. She warned, "People easily get these bacteria at Thanksgiving by eating dressing insufficiently cooked inside the turkey. The bacteria are vicious. For the first twenty-four hours, you're afraid you're going to die. For the next twenty-four hours, you're afraid you *aren't* going to die."

Caleb also signed up for English composition, political science, chemistry, college algebra, botany, psychology, and trigonometry. He enjoyed all but the last two. Psychology lecture was in a large, ell-shaped room, where from some seats in the back, one couldn't even see the lecturing professor, who was boring anyway. Caleb thought the subject matter was trivial, subjective, even incomprehensible.

In trigonometry, his scores on the daily quizzes were barely passing. "I memorize all the rules and definitions of secant, cosine, tangent, etc., every night, but overnight, the Greek gods shuffle the cards so what I learned isn't so any longer." After tanking all the quizzes, he dropped the course on the last day possible. After dropping trig, he had only eleven hours; that quarter was his lowest gpa, only 3.0 out of possible 4.0, not spectacular but okay.

Caleb enjoyed his life as a student. He palled around with three other freshmen in his dorm. During Orientation Week, before classes began, they went to the movies three nights; once classes began, they realized they needed to study; midweek movies ceased. The four went together to football games, though the Cougars were abysmally poor, and to basketball games in the Smith Fieldhouse.

Early in fall quarter, he joined Kia Ora Club, made up of Polynesian students, returned missionaries from New Zealand, and a few others. The members of Kia Ora Club learned Maori chants and dances to perform them for various ward socials in the communities around BYU.

The men each wore a *piupiu*, a grass skirt, over undershorts, the last for modesty. They painted bare chests, legs, and faces with grease-paint copies of Maori tattoos.

On one night, there were warnings from older members: "Make sure you sleep in pajamas tonight." At 5:00 AM the next day, members were awakened and summoned to a "Come As You Are" breakfast party.

Wearing pajamas in mixed company was not in keeping with the moral attitudes of BYU administrators. Wearing pajamas was, of course, much more acceptable than what some men might have been wearing without the warning the night before. This party got the Kia Ora Club in trouble with the university. A new regulation came out: pajama parties were not acceptable.

Thus, two years passed with Caleb having a great time, loving Provo, building friendships, with no firm ideas on a major. He also found himself quite attracted to male friends, especially a

150

junior in Kia Ora Club. When Caleb
realized his attraction was homosexual, he
broke off the friendship with harsh words
to the other man.

2
"Language and Literature"

Wants pawn term dare
worsted ladle gull hoe lift
wetter murder inner ladle
cordage honor itch offer
lodge, dock, florist. Disk
ladle gull orphan worry
putty ladle rat cluck wetter
ladle rat hut, an fur disk
raisin pimple colder Ladle
Rat Rotten Hut.[1]

---

1   *Anguish Languish* by Howard L. Chase at
Project Gutenberg, Urbana, Illinois, in section,
"Furry Tells" on its website,
https://www.gutenberg.org/ebooks/64432.
This site indicates that *Anguish Languish* is in
"public domain," not protected by copyright.

       On a visit to the Project Gutenberg site
on 15 January 2022, the wording indicated that "It
is always OK to cite Project Gutenberg as the
publication source,..., and it is also OK to not cite
Project Gutenberg: your choice."

Caleb first heard this version of the fairy tale in an English class. He was so entranced that he remembered some of the lines for decades afterwards. Although he was more enchanted with language than with anything else, Miss Morrell, who taught his freshman writing class, had a tremendous influence even before he heard the fairy tale. The first day of class, she walked into the classroom so smoothly, so beautifully. Then she spoke, and he fell in love—with sounds. After two quarters of her composition courses, he registered for a lower-level Shakespeare course she taught. Then Shakespeare —especially the poetry between Romeo and Juliet—captivated him.

Over the years at the "Y," in literature classes poetry reverberated. He "heard" the music as he read Paton's opening lines of a "road that runs from Ixopo into the hills." Austen's opening paragraph that "a single man" newly arrived in the neighborhood and "in possession of a fortune must be in want of a wife" captivated him several times; he reread *Pride and Prejudice* each time.

He cut out a series of "Pogo" which depended on suprasegmental phonemes to carry the double entendres, then shared them with the professor of the History of English Language course he was taking at the time. The comic strip "Pogo" illustrated other aspects of language as well and delighted Caleb with its imagery and symbolic cartooning. Perhaps his favorite was Kelly's mole, a blind member of the Okefenokee Swamp community whose ultra-conservative ideas and spoken words were written in gothic type face. He also loved Kelly's takes on Christmas songs, "Deck the Halls" and "The Twelve Days of Christmas." *Someone really ought to publish the complete works of Walt Kelly,* he reflected often.

In later undergraduate years, English literature occupied most of Caleb's time; he signed up for period survey courses and focus courses on individual writers and specific genres. In

154

his Chaucer class, he received a nickname, "the clerke," when Professor McKendrick greeted him by quoting from *Canterbury Tales,* "Gladly wolde he learne and gladly teache." Eventually Caleb focused on Victorian literature, particularly the novels of George Elliott and the poetry of Gerard Manley Hopkins, but even with such emphasis in his classes, Caleb did not officially declare English his major until the beginning of his last semester for his BA.

3
"'El Misionero'"

Mormon society expects that young Mormon men will take time off from their studies or work to serve as missionaries. During his freshman year at the "Y," the Church changed the age at which young men could go on missions from twenty-one to nineteen. Many men altered their plans to go on their mission that summer. Caleb did not.

Instead, Caleb attended summer school. That summer he met an older man, Bob, who taught art in a high school in Arizona and studied at BYU each summer. He admired Bob. Bob enjoyed life and sex. When they walked across campus, Bob talked to Caleb about the contours of the women's bodies–not just as a man but also as an artist. As they talked, Caleb recognized he had never looked at girls with that kind of interest.

Caleb registered for classes for fall semester and then for spring semester. He continued enjoying most of his classes and his social life with friends. He continued his study of Spanish and chemistry. The newer topics he enjoyed included political science.

BYU moved to the semester system that year. As a result of combining trigonometry with college algebra in the new system, Caleb would have to repeat trigonometry in the combined new course in order to continue studying chemistry. He decided against chemistry.

At the end of spring semester 1961, Caleb didn't know what to do. He was tired of school; he didn't want to get a job that would only pass time before he would return, sooner or later, to the "Y." He couldn't consider travel; he had no money, nor did his family. When Bob came back to the "Y" for summer school, Caleb went to see him and shared with him his confusion as to what to do.

"Why don't you go on a mission?"
Bob asked.

Yes! That's what I want to do,
Caleb realized. *I'll do just that.*

Caleb went about volunteering
quietly. He approached the bishop of his
Draper ward without telling anyone in the
family. He asked the bishop to keep it
secret even from CT who was a close
friend of the bishop. During this interview
he confessed that he found men attractive,
explaining why he didn't want anyone
else to know he was asking for a mission
call. His bishop listened, then promised
him in a blessing that the Lord would take
away those feelings if he served an
honorable mission. *Missionary service
will finally resolve this terrible attraction,*
he reasoned.

Caleb filled out the request form
the bishop had and set up an interview
with the stake president. After the latter
interview, he had the forms mailed to Salt
Lake City and told his parents and
Maryelle, and told them not to tell anyone

158

until his call came. Then they waited. And waited.

Later, a cousin, a grandson of Aunt Mary and Uncle Brigham, started his process and told everyone about it. The letter calling his cousin to Argentina came and the entire extended family rejoiced. Caleb and his family continued to wait in silence.

Finally the letter came. Caleb was called to missionary service in the West Spanish American mission of the Church, with headquarters in East Los Angeles, California. Though he was disappointed not to be going to Latin America, he kept his disappointment silently, not telling anyone.

The family rejoiced. CT was proud that his son was to become a missionary. After CT had become active in the Church, he regretted he had not gone on a mission; when he was young and single, he had had no interest at all in serving as a missionary.

Emma was happy, proud, vindicated in her heart that her son was now going on a mission. Caleb was the only young man his age in the ward who had not become a missionary. Now the Sunday smugness of the mothers of missionaries in their ward would disappear, or at least lessen.

Maryelle was thrilled. She had served a mission and returned home two years previously.

Caleb would enter the mission home in downtown Salt Lake City for the usual week-long indoctrination period in late October. A week later, his parents and Maryelle drove him to the Union Pacific train station to catch the train to Los Angeles.

No other missionaries and families were at the station. When boarding time came, Caleb hugged his mother. "I'll miss you, mom."

"I will miss you. I'm very proud of you. Do well." She cried.

160

Shaking hands with his father, then hugging him, Caleb said, "Dad, I love you. I'll do well. Promise."

"We're all proud of you and love you deeply. Write as often as you are allowed, especially to your mother."

"I can only write once a week, probably Sunday or Monday afternoons, but I'll write."

"Goodbye, Ellie, Maryelle," he said teasing her with his nickname for her, switching to the name she preferred. He hugged her.

After having spent a week in the mission home constantly with a companion, he felt acutely alone. After supper in the dining car, he walked to the dome car where he sat looking at the dark night and at the headlight of the locomotive swinging back and forth across the railroad right of way.

He returned to his seat in the coach ahead of the dome car. Everyone in

161

the darkened car slept. Caleb sat down, turned toward the window and closed his eyes.

About three o'clock next afternoon, the conductor came through the coaches announcing the imminent arrival of the train in East Los Angeles. Caleb got his suitcase and briefcase and stood in the vestibule, ready to disembark. When the train stopped in East LA, Caleb got off. A few people stood on the platform, waiting for arrivals. One by one, group by group, they met their parties and left. When Caleb remained alone on the platform, he went inside to the ticket agent.

"Where can I find a telephone to call the people who should be meeting me?" he asked.

"The telephones are by the restrooms," he answered, nodding to the sign "Restrooms Telephones" above an entrance to a hallway off the waiting room.

162

"Thank you. I guess I'm a little blind."

Caleb crossed the waiting room to the telephones, found a dime in his pocket, inserted it in the slot and waited. "Please deposit twenty cents," a recorded voice sounded in his ear.

He found another dime in his pocket, inserted it and got a dial tone. He dialed the number of the mission home he received before he left Salt Lake City.

A woman answered the telephone, "West Spanish American Mission, Sister Ramos speaking."

"Hi, I'm Elder Reynolds. I'm at the station and nobody is here to meet me. How do I get to the mission home?"

"Oh, my goodness. You're here already? Someone will come right away to pick you up. Just stay there. Someone will be there in about ten minutes."

4
"East Los Angeles Mission Home"

When the missionaries and Caleb arrived at the mission home, President Brunson asked Caleb to come into his office for a short interview to get to know him. "Sit down," he said to Caleb.

"¿Cómo estaba el viaje?" he began.

"Uh. Did you ask how the journey was?"

"En Español, por favor."

"El viaje fué bueno." Caleb responded.

"¿Se encontraron Vd a álgien?"

"Uh. Por favor, repite Vd." Caleb said.

164

"¿Se encontraron Vd.... Le conocieron Vd a álguien nuevo?"

"Si me preguntaron Vd. si hablé yo con álguien, sí, hablé con una mujer cuando comimos la cena en el "dining car." Caleb answered, stabbing at the president's meaning.

"Muy bien," President Brunson complimented Caleb. "You do fairly well with Spanish, but you must study regularly. We will provide you with a small grammar primer you should study during the first couple of weeks. When you finish with it, we can send you other books on Spanish. We also will equip you with the lesson plans we use and expect you to memorize these lessons in Spanish. Your companion will work with you on the lessons, helping you prepare to use these lessons with investigators.

"If you have lesson plans in English, throw them away. We don't want you spending time learning English language materials. Although at times you will have to teach in English, you already

165

know the language. Spend your study
time mastering Spanish.

"We encourage the missionaries to
read the Book of Mormon aloud in
Spanish to learn the sounds of the
language as well as the gospel doctrine.
It's important to hear your own
pronunciation to improve it.

"I also have here a small book of
mission regulations we've compiled. You
should read this over every month or so,
just to refresh your memory. Among other
items, it talks about contacts with friends
and family. You can write your parents
once a week. That's the extent of contact
with home. Also, one letter per month,
not per week, to a girlfriend if you've left
one at home. You are also to be with your
companion at all times. Except to shower,
bathe, or go to the bathroom, you should
be in the same room as he is.

"We usually keep missionaries
here for a week. However, I'm thinking of
sending you out tomorrow to Phoenix. Is
that okay with you?"

166

"Yes." *Why wouldn't I be okay with that? Do I have a say in this? I thought I was expected to obey, not dissent. Well, I really am okay with that decision.*

"Supper will be served in the dining room at 6:30. In the meantime, you can go to the rooms above the garage where you will sleep tonight. I'll have one of the elders in the office take you there." So ended the interview.

The missionaries stationed at the Mission Home gathered for supper at 6:30 PM. The formal dining room in the home on Via Corona Street held a table at which President Brunson, three children, six missionaries counting Elder Reynolds, sat. With two other place settings with chairs still empty arranged around it, they were a little squished for space. The hired housekeeper/cook and sister Brunson carried the serving dishes in from the kitchen, then sat down.

President Brunson said the blessing, and everyone began passing the

167

main food dishes around, serving themselves as the dishes arrived. After the vegetables, meat, and potatoes had circulated, people began to eat,

"Elder Beesom," President Brunson addressed his assistant, "According to our plans, you are taking Elder Reynolds to Phoenix tomorrow. What time do you plan to leave here?"

"Well," Elder Beesom responded, "it will take us about eight hours to drive there, so I think we should leave no later than 8:00 AM. That'll get us to the Elders' apartment around five o'clock or so, depending upon traffic. I don't want to be so late that the Elders there may have gone out for evening appointments after their supper."

"I'll telephone them tomorrow morning about seven so they know when to expect you," President Brunson said. "Elder Reynolds, as I said in our meeting earlier, we usually keep new missionaries here for about a week for instruction and some really basic language training, but

168

our interview confirmed the information the Church has sent us that you've already studied Spanish in college, so we're skipping the normal stay in your case. Are you ready for travel?"

"Sure."

After dessert, President Brunson said, "Elder Reynolds, the missionaries who stay in the mission home have the responsibility of washing dishes after each meal. They rotate that among themselves, but I'm asking you to join the two who wash up tonight and again after breakfast tomorrow morning."

5
"Phoenix"

Washington Street was the main highway leading into Phoenix from the west and onto Tempe and Mesa east of Phoenix. Traveling east on Washington from downtown, the elders quickly entered one of the barrios of Phoenix, neighborhoods in which Mexican Americans settled.

When they crossed 20th Street, Elder Beesom turned right into the third driveway beside a small stucco house. Behind the house, the driveway widened in front of a row of three cottages, where parking for the renters existed. Trees lined the west side of the driveway; the patches of lawn were dull greenish brown at the end of a hot summer. The Elders lived in the cottage closest to the landlord's house in the front.

Elder Beesom parked the car next to the small foreign car belonging to the

170

senior companion who lived here. The elders climbed out of the car.

"Elder Anderson, this is Elder Reynolds," Elder Beesom began when the elders living in the cottage invited them inside. "Elder White, Elder Reynolds."

"Pleased to meet you," Elder Anderson said to Elder Reynolds. "How was your journey?" he asked Elder Beesom.

"Not bad," Elder Beesom said. "We made it in just over eight hours."

"Do you have any appointments for tonight?" Elder Beesom asked.

"Well, we want to go by the Vegas family so Elder White can say goodbye before you take him tomorrow morning to Yuma," Elder Anderson said. "You're welcome to come with us or stay here."

"Well, it would be a good idea for Elder Reynolds to go also, wouldn't it, so he could meet the Vegases as well. But I will stay here by myself."

Elders Anderson, White, and Reynolds left to visit the Vegas family, and Elder Beesom relaxed, took a shower, and went to bed in one of the extra cots the elders had borrowed for this night.

That night when the elders returned to the cottage, Elder Reynolds wondered where he would sleep. He saw one large bed and Elder Beesom asleep in a cot near the wall opposite the bed.

Elder Anderson answered his question, "There's a cot folded up against the wall next to the bathroom door. You can set that up along the same wall as Elder Beesom's cot. We will have a group prayer once we're ready for bed. Don't unpack tonight; you can do that tomorrow."

I guess Elder White and Elder Anderson both sleep in the same bed. Hmm.

172

The next morning was quite hectic with four men needing to use the small bathroom. Elder Beesom's decision to shower and shave the night before saved time. After shaving and showering, Elder White quickly gathered his belongings; they left at 8:00 o'clock.

"Well, tell me about yourself," Elder Anderson said as soon as the other elders left.

"I grew up in Draper, Utah, at the south end of Salt Lake County. I have an older sister, Mary Louise, but we call her Maryelle. Dad owns a small business in Sandy, a neighboring town more toward Salt Lake City. When I was really young, he worked in a feed store in Draper. We have a pasture where we fatten a yearling calf each summer and we have a few ewes so we can have lambs for slaughter each fall. We also have a dozen hens we keep for eggs. When one of the hens gets setting, we buy a dozen chicks for her. I get to slaughter the roosters when they're big enough for frying," he said stressing "get to" with irony.

"After high school, I went to BYU for a couple of years. There I took second year Spanish, so I guess that's why I got called here."

"Entonces, habla Vd. Español. ¡Qué bueno!"

"Sí, puedo hablar un poco." Elder Reynolds responded.

"Esta mañana podemos ir a casas donde la gente nos invitamos a regressar."

"Perdóneme. No entiendo,"

"I said, 'This morning we can go to a few places where Elder White and I were invited to return to visit them later.' But we really have too many other, more important things to do today.

"We should set up regular study time when we converse in Spanish, and time when I will listen to you read in Spanish from *El Libro de Mormon*. We can set up an hour and a half for study each morning after breakfast, from about 7:30 to 9:00.

"You should plan to have about an hour of that time for your individual study, then we'll spend fifteen minutes of you reading aloud in Spanish to me and fifteen minutes of Spanish conversation about the Gospel, about our work, the families we visit, or just generally about Phoenix. This way you will learn to understand Spanish.

"Then we will go out contacting people."

During the day, the elders also packed the two cots into the car and took them back to the Ventura family from whom they had borrowed them. *Well, we sleep together,* Elder Reynolds thought. *Why does that make any difference? It's scary, but....*

Two nights later, Elder Reynolds woke up, needing to go to the bathroom. When he returned to the bed, he lay still for a few minutes before falling asleep

175

again. *Uh? Oh,* he thought when Elder Anderson, while rolling over, moved his foot against Elder Reynold's foot. Elder Reynolds immediately moved his foot away. *Oh, I wish I hadn't done that. I hope Elder Anderson won't be offended. But I couldn't leave my foot there against his foot. He'd think I was homosexual.*

The first Sunday in Phoenix Thirteenth Ward, the Spanish-speaking ward which the elders always attended, he met many members of the Church and the four elders who were temporarily working in the Phoenix area from the West Mexican Mission in Sonora, Mexico. From the beginning, Elder Reynolds related fairly well with members of the church. He spoke his limited Spanish to them, and listened intently to their words to him, although he often had to ask them to repeat what they had said to be certain he understood.

The members helped him by encouraging him, speaking Spanish to him, and complementing him. He enjoyed his increasing skill, loved the approbation

176

the members gave him as his skill improved. He related easily with married people, but he felt awkward with teenagers and single adults in their early twenties.

In their regular work, the elders frequently met with member families. As they became friends with members, the missionaries asked if they knew friends or neighbors who might be interested in hearing about the Church. When members gave the elders names of people, they would contact them in their homes to see if they would be interested in hearing about the Mormon church. While most were not interested, those who did indicate an interest became the best investigators. Many of these referrals were baptized in the months after the elders first contacted them.

"Tracting," walking through a neighborhood, knocking on each door and talking to anyone who answered, was much less successful; very few of these contacts joined the church.

At the beginning of his mission, Elder Reynolds had little confidence with the non-Mormon Mexicans they met. He was quiet, unsure, even when meeting referrals from church members, but once a contact showed some interest in hearing messages about the Mormon Church, Elder Reynolds gradually relaxed and began trying to carry on conversations.

During the first week in Phoenix, he saw the first of many blessings to come to him as the result of other missionaries' efforts. The night of his second day in Phoenix, the elders returned to the Vegas family. Elders Anderson and White had been teaching the Vegases for over three months. That night, as Elders Anderson and Reynolds were walking back to the car, Elder Anderson asked Ricky Vegas if he wanted to be baptized on Saturday. When Ricky said yes, the elders returned to the house to ask his mother for her permission. That night, Elder Reynolds wrote in his journal.

Ricky said yes, he
wanted to be baptized. We

178

went back to talk to Sister
Vegas, and she asked to be
baptized as well. By the
time we left, Sister Vegas,
Ricky, Juan, and Elisa said
they wanted to be baptized.
María and José also said
they want to join the
church, but they need more
time. Wow! I'm so happy!

As part of their work, the elders
attended MIA, the youth auxiliary of the
church, on Tuesday evenings. When the
class sessions for the youth were over, the
elders joined them in bowling. When they
had investigators between ages twelve
and twenty-something, they invited them
to MIA and bowling. The elders from the
West Mexican Mission, Elders Anderson
and Reynolds, and the youth from the
ward and their friends made enough for
three, sometimes four teams.

Elder Reynolds noticed the good
looks of some of the teenagers. *Becky is
so cute, I could hug her. That wouldn't
do. Someone would misunderstand. But,*

I'd like to, she's so cute. One evening when two investigators, who were cousins of a member girl, first came bowling, Elder Reynolds noticed the form and skill of the one who was on the same team as he was. *He is so good looking. His jeans show off his body. He looks so smooth as he lets go of the ball. Oh, my. Now Caleb,* he scolded himself.

As time passed, Elder Reynolds learned about Elder Anderson. He and his brothers and father hunted every year in Montana where they lived. One year they traveled to Alaska to hunt where they had shot a Dahl Sheep and two elk.

Elder Reynolds had never previously wanted to go hunting. *I'd like to go hunting with him. I don't want to kill anything and have to clean it, but. . . . Fish are okay; chickens, not so good; a deer would make me gag.*

Elder Anderson played football and basketball in his small high school and loved playing basketball with other missionaries on their diversion/cleanup

180

day. On diversion day, Elder Reynolds
joined in; he was okay, but not very
assertive. He did not drive for the basket
even against elders his size but preferred
to shoot from outside when he could
shake off the man guarding him. After
their first diversion day, Elder Anderson
didn't say anything about their basketball
experience. Over the weeks, Elder
Reynolds worked harder at basketball and
did better.

One day Elder Anderson said,
"You did quite well today in basketball. I
like the way you attacked the basket
against Elder Larson."

"Thanks," Elder Reynolds
muttered and smiled. *I did real well. I
enjoyed going body to body against him.
Yeah, and I scored!*

One evening when the full moon
was just rising over the Superstition
Mountains, it appeared reddish from the
dust in the air. Elders Anderson and
Reynolds were driving to an appointment.

"Wow; the moon is bloody," Elder Reynolds commented.

"Yeah. Time for vampires," Elder Anderson responded, still looking straight ahead while driving.

"Tch, tch, tch, tch," Elder Reynolds said, trying to imitate the sound of a bat. "Oh, man. The look you had on your face. Your eyes were so wide open. I sure had you fooled."

Elder Anderson laughed. "Yeah, you definitely got me," and he gave Elder Reynolds a friendly punch.

Oh, golly. It's great to have him slug me. He really likes me.

One night in the apartment, Elder Reynolds told Elder Anderson that his grandmother was a Taylor, one of the daughters of the counselor to the president of the Church. "My father goes by 'CT,' but his middle name is 'Taylor' in honor of my great-grandfather."

"Which Taylor was he?"

"He was counselor to the president of the Church. His uncle was President John Taylor."

"Wow," Elder Anderson responded with genuine admiration.

After six months in Phoenix, Elder Reynolds got a letter from President Brunson transferring him to Yuma where he would work with Elder Johnson. Elder Young, the president's assistant after Elder Beesom went home, would bring Elder Anderson's new companion on a Tuesday and take Elder Reynolds the next day to Yuma.

At MIA that night, Elder Anderson spoke to all the youth just before they left the church to go bowling. "Tonight is Elder Reynolds' last night with us. He's being transferred to Yuma tomorrow morning. I want everyone to know what a great guy he's been; he's been a hard worker and a good companion. If any of you have a favorite

memory of something you did together,
let him know."

Several of the youth spoke one on
one to Elder Reynolds that night telling
him of their appreciation.

"I love you," Elder Reynolds
responded. "Thanks for helping us do our
work here in Phoenix. You've been a
great help to me."

6
"Larkin Family"

During the months Elder Reynolds was assigned to Phoenix, he had significant experiences with two families. The Larkin family worked closely with the elders. Brother Larkin frequently acted as the non-missionary Church authority who interviewed baptismal candidates, verifying their preparedness to accept membership in the Church. The day after Elders Anderson and Reynolds visited the Vegas family and got their commitment to be baptized, the elders planned to return to the Vegas family home with Brother Larkin to interview those who wanted to be baptized that weekend. The plans changed slightly when Elder Reynolds came down with diarrhea and nausea, vomiting his breakfast.

As Elder Anderson had a doctor appointment he needed to keep, Elder Reynolds climbed into the back seat of Elder Anderson's little car and slept. After attending to the few errands Elder Anderson needed to do, he drove to the Larkins' home. Right away, Sister Larkin took Elder Reynolds' temperature which was high, gave him orange juice, and put him to bed. Elder Anderson and Brother Larkin went at the scheduled time to interview the Vegas family members who wanted to be baptized.

When Brother Larkin and Elder Anderson returned, Elder Anderson wished to awaken Elder Reynolds so they could go home, but he passed out in the Larkins' living room. He had a high fever and was sick for three days. The two missionaries stayed with the Larkins the entire time. After experiencing the compassion and attentive care the Larkins gave them, Elder Reynolds felt close to the Larkin family.

During these three days with the Larkin family, he asked Sister Larkin how she had met Brother Larkin.

Sister Larkin, nee Hernandez, was raised in the church by her grandmother in

186

rural New Mexico. When the missionary who taught Sister Larkin's grandmother returned as mission president almost thirty years later, He and his wife invited Sister Larkin, who was in her early twenties, to move to the mission home in San Antonio, Texas, so she could more easily find employment. She was living there when Brother Larkin came as a missionary to the Spanish American Mission

Near the end of his mission, Elder Larkin was assigned for two months to live at the mission home and work with the president. At the end of his mission, he asked the mission president if it would be acceptable if he returned to San Antonio to date Sister Hernandez. The mission president approved. Elder Larkin went home to Logan for a short while, then returned to court María. They married in the Mesa, Arizona, Temple so María's grandmother could attend as well as his family. Then they moved to Logan so Elder Larkin could resume his studies at the "AC."[2]

Shortly after Elder Reynolds told Elder Anderson that his father's middle name was Taylor, one evening at the Larkins' home, Elder Anderson said to everyone in the living room, "Elder, tell the Larkins what your father's middle name is and why."

"Oh, it's just 'T,'" Elder Reynolds lied, embarrassed because he felt talking about his genealogy would be bragging. He didn't recognize that his telling Elder Anderson in the first place was boasting; he had wanted to gain prestige in Elder Anderson's eyes, the very thing he now tried to prevent by refusing to tell the truth. He didn't acknowledge his initial bragging, nor did he apologize later to Elder Anderson for embarrassing him.

Despite the awkwardness caused by Elder Reynolds' white lie, Elder

---

2   Utah State Agriculture College, since 1957, Utah State University.

Anderson continued mentoring Elder Reynolds; the Larkins continued helping him, growing to love him. In January, Elder Reynolds wrote in his journal of an event Sister Larkin had recently experienced:

> Tonight, after MIA, we went to the Larkins' for a short visit. Sister Larkin shared with us a telephone conversation she had the night before. She had telephoned the stake Young Women's president to ask the date and time of the stake Gold and Green Ball so she could announce it in MIA on Tuesday. She introduced herself—Sister Larkin of the Phoenix Thirteenth Ward—and asked her question. "Oh," came the answer, "We don't want the Mexicans to come!"

Sister Larkin stayed silent, then said, "I am Mexican."

"Oh, I'm sorry, I didn't mean to offend," was the stammered reply. "Please don't take this personally."

How else could Sister Larkin take it? I don't understand what Church members have against *Mejicanos*. They're Lamanites, descendants of the Book of Mormon people, and children of Israel. It's just wrong!

This was not the first time Elder Reynolds experienced anti-Mexican sentiment in the church, but it was the first during his mission and one that made an impression he never forgot.

7
"Muñoz Family"

The other family who made a major impact on Elder Reynolds were the Muñozes, a non-member family. About three months after Elder Reynolds began his mission, the elders received a referral from a member to visit the Muñoz family, recent immigrants from Mexico who spoke no English. They had a baby girl. They spoke sophisticated Spanish, suggesting they were well educated.

The lessons the elders presented to the Muñoz family continued for six weeks or so. As Elder Reynolds worked at understanding Brother Muñoz' Spanish so he could talk to him more easily, they became some of Elder Reynolds' favorite contacts. Listening to their beautiful Spanish, trying to understand their comments, he realized he was learning a more sophisticated Spanish.

In his journal, Elder Reynolds wrote of his progress in speaking and comprehending Spanish. After meeting with the Muñoz family a few times, Elder Reynolds wrote of a specific experience with the Muñoz family.

Last night I had a beautiful experience with the Muñoz family. When we arrived, I had the usual struggle understanding everything they said and could usually guess at a few words and after hearing what they said again, could repeat to them what I thought they said. It was usually right. Then I'd answer, and we'd go on.

During the lesson, Elder Anderson asked Brother Muñoz the questions, and I understood his answers. Elder presented more of the discussion and then asked another question. I understood the question and Brother Muñoz's answer. I understood everything he said when he said it. I understood the closing prayer. But then while Elder Anderson set up an appointment for our next visit, I couldn't understand everything Brother Muñoz said.

When we got to the car and I sat down in the front seat, I realized what had happened. I was stunned. Throughout the lesson, I understood everything, but before and after the lesson I didn't understand the conversations. The Lord blessed me with the gift of tongues: I understood Brother Muñoz' Spanish, and if I continue to work at it, the Lord will bless me

that I can speak and
understand Spanish. I am
so grateful for this
blessing.

After presenting six lessons on the
Mormon Church to the Muñoz family,
Brother Muñoz said that they were no
longer interested in taking more lessons
nor in joining the church.

8
"Elders in Los Angeles"

After only two weeks in Yuma,
Elder Reynolds received another transfer.
He was reassigned to work as the junior
companion to Elder Shurtz in one of the
barrios of Los Angeles. It was not a happy
assignment. Elder Reynolds thought Elder
Shurtz was too lazy. They didn't spend
full days proselytizing, tracting, etc. Elder
Reynolds seemed to have forgotten that
he and Elder Anderson tracted only
occasionally. None of the people they met
expressed real interest in learning about
the Mormon Church.

When Elder Reynolds contrasted
these two companions, Elder Shurtz came
up short.

In his journal Elder Reynolds
wrote his opinion frankly:

Elder is so trunky.
He just wants to go home

and he's still got five
months to go. We don't
have any real investigators.
Instead, we visit Sister
Gonzalez, a member who
isn't active. She's young,
single, and good looking.
And she likes him to come
visit. We don't visit other
inactive members nor any
of the active members.

Day before
yesterday, I told Elder
Shurtz that in Phoenix,
Elder Anderson and I
would go bowling every
Tuesday night with the
youth group after MIA
class. Well, Elder Shurtz
liked that idea so today
when we visited Sister
Gonzalez, he invited her to
go bowling with us
tomorrow night. Just the
three of us. I don't think
this is very good
missionary work. We

aren't going with other
members of the church. It
isn't helping her get to
know other members.

The following week, Elder
Reynolds wrote again about bowling with
Sister Gonzalez:

I've never been so
lucky. I got some strikes
and picked up most of the
spares. This was the first
time I ever scored above
150; in the second game I
got 180! And I beat Elder
Shurtz both games.

They didn't go bowling again.

After two and a half months with
Elder Shurtz, Elder Reynolds received
another transfer. By this time in his
mission, Elder Reynolds felt he was ready
to be senior companion. He had learned
the standardized missionary discussions.
He had read *El Libro de Mormon* once

and was well into "2° Nefi" a second time through. He spoke Spanish fairly well.

He was not made senior, however; he was assigned as companion to Elder Norman who was about to be released at the end of his thirty months as a missionary. Elder Norman was a quiet man, soft spoken, no longer as energetic as a new missionary. Elder Reynolds treated Elder Norman with slight disparagement, thinking of Elder Norman in the terms of the passage in Revelations 3:15-16 as "neither hot nor cold, but to be spewed out of one's mouth."

Upon Elder Norman's release, Elder Reynolds received his new assignment. He would be senior companion in the Imperial Valley of southern California. They would live in Brawley, but cover the *Mejicanos* in all the towns from Calexico on the border to the Salton Sea. He would be in charge of arranging their work; he was supposed to know what to do. Elder Reynolds panicked:

198

What will I do? How do I get to know the area? I haven't an idea what to do. I'm floundering, like a fish on land.

He wanted Elder Richards, who was a new missionary, to look up to him as a good senior companion, to like him. *What is he thinking about me,* Elder Reynolds worried. Gradually, Elder Reynolds realized how poorly he had treated Elder Norman. Some weeks later, Caleb recorded in his journal his re-evaluation of Elder Norman and his time with him:

> I realize now how unkind I was to Elder Norman. When I was transferred to him, I had expected to be made senior....

> But I was assigned to Elder Norman for his last six weeks. I know I was mean to him. I didn't argue with him, I just assented to his plans, but I

was angry. I know he
could tell, and he tried. He
was so willing to hear what
I thought we should do; It
didn't get him anywhere
with me. I should write to
him apologizing for my
attitude. I wish I had been
nicer to him.

9
"Budding Social Conscience"

Sister Larkin's sharing her experience in Phoenix with Elders Anderson and Reynolds marked the first real beginning of Elder Reynolds' social conscience. In Los Angeles seven or so months later, he had a conversation with two other missionaries which further reveals his evolving social conscience.

One evening, Elder Reynolds and two other missionaries talked about their relations with members. Elder Jenkins mentioned his attraction to one of the young women in the Spanish ward they attended. Elder Peterson said getting involved with a *Mejicana* was as bad as getting involved with a Negro girl.

Elder Jenkins argued back that Mexicans could hold the priesthood so there was not similarity. Elder Peterson still insisted that it was just as bad.

As they argued opinions Elder Reynolds remained silent, then said, "I'd prefer my sister to marry a good *Mejicano* or even a Negro man than a cruel white member of the church."

"You're crazy!" Elder Jenkins said.

"They couldn't marry in the temple. Their kids couldn't hold the priesthood," Elder Peterson said.

"I still think she'd be better off with a good Negro man who loved her and treated her kindly than with a white man who abused her."

"An abusive man couldn't take her to the temple either. Active members aren't abusive," Elder Jenkins responded.

"Oh, come now," put in Elder Peterson. "I know several men who are active and cruel to others, even abusive."

Hearing their reactions, Elder Reynolds remained silent.

202

Months later, after working in the Imperial Valley, Elder Reynolds was sent to rural Arizona. He and his companion received a referral from a Mexican member family to visit a Lopez family living west of Buckeye. Out there the county roads run north to south and east to west, intersecting every mile. The Lopezes lived in one of several shacks, each inhabited by a family or group of single men, beside a dirt driveway turning off one of the county roads, just after a crossroads. They invited the elders into their home.

Inside, the shack stood two double beds, stretching almost wall to wall on opposite sides of the room. A small table at the foot of one bed held a two-burner hot plate on which Sister Lopez cooked meals. The family of seven ate off a fold-up table, set up at mealtime, between the two beds. At night, the four older children slept in one bed; Brother and Sister Lopez and the baby slept in the other bed.

Both Brother and Sister Lopez worked in the fields of the *patron,* picking

203

cotton, dragging long heavy canvas bags behind them as they picked the bolls from the dried plants and stuffed them into the bags. The dried cotton plants were sturdy and sharp, scratching unprotected hands and arms. In addition to dragging her canvas bag, Sister Lopez often carried the baby on her back while picking cotton. Even though it was November, daytime temperatures frequently hit the high nineties.

About a month after beginning to teach the Lopez family, the elders received another referral, this time from one of the stake high counselors in the Phoenix West Stake. In his journal, Elder Reynolds described his feelings upon meeting the Diaz family.

While I was working in Brawley, I excused the big difference between the owners' homes and the workers' homes by thinking the owners weren't members of the church. They didn't

know the true Gospel.
Here, Brother Smithson is
on the stake high council.
He obviously should know
the gospel. But his workers
live in the same kind of
houses as the Lopez
family. He sent us to meet
one of his workers, Brother
Diaz, and his family.

Their house stands
alone in a field, no other
houses around. The house
has a dirt floor. There is no
running water and no
swamp cooler. Brother
Smithson lives in a brick
home with five bedrooms,
three bathrooms, central
air conditioning, and a
three-car garage. The Book
of Mormon says in Zion
there were no poor among
the inhabitants; all were
equal. Brother Smithson
should use his wealth to

improve his workers' lives.
This isn't right.

10
"Adjustments"

Near the end of his mission, Elder Reynolds received an unusual assignment. By this time, he was a zone leader, in charge of several pairs of missionaries working in separate areas. He was not assigned a junior companion, however, but to be the companion of another elder who was nearing the end of his mission. Elder Case was designated senior companion, in charge of the work in their specific area. As supervisor of other missionaries in the zone, Elder Reynolds sometimes needed to visit a pair of them. That work as zone leader would take precedence. Otherwise, Elder Case would plan their work and activities in the area.

Elder Case presented Elder Reynolds with a problem, one he himself faced: how to stay focused on missionary work when nearing the end of one's mission. He recorded his frustration in his journal:

When Elder Case
and I became companions,
the president made it clear
that I would be zone
leader, but Elder Case
would be senior, in charge
of our work in the area. So,
unless I have zone
business, he makes the
arrangements for our days.
We do nothing. Last week
in my monthly report, I
recorded only those hours I
felt we had put into
missionary work in our
area: thirty-two for the
whole month. As all the
other missionaries in the
zone see all our hours, that
didn't sit well with Elder
Case.

After two months with this
arrangement, Elder Reynolds wrote to the
mission president. The president sent his
two assistants to visit Elders Reynolds
and Case. One assistant, Elder Jones, had
been good friends with Elder Reynolds

since early in their missions. Elder Jones sent his companion with Elder Case to visit some contacts, and then Elders Jones and Reynolds sat in the car and talked.

"Elder Reynolds," Elder Jones began, "President Brunson is concerned that this experience with Elder Case might spoil your mission. If this assignment lasts through the end of your mission, will you still consider your mission experience positive?"

"Put that way, yes. This is only for a few more weeks before I'm released. I realize it's only temporary. And I have had some wonderful experiences during the mission."

"You have been a good missionary. You've had numerous baptisms. You've touched the lives of many members and non-members. I'm happy that you can see this, and that you won't let this final assignment ruin your mission experience."

"No, no. It won't. But I'll still be extra happy to be released."

And he was. In the months following his release while attending summer school and fall semester at BYU, other recently returned missionaries frequently expressed their wish that they were still back in the mission field.

"Oh, I don't want to be back!" Caleb always said. "I'm so grateful to be home. President McKay would have to tell me personally to go back before I would return."

After his mission, Caleb slacked off on his journal writing, but he still wrote on occasion. Several months after his mission, in the fall of 1964, he enrolled in the Shakespeare course for English majors at BYU. He wrote in his journal a diatribe about the professor:

> Today, Professor
> Christiansen said that it
> was a shame that the
> United States was the only

first-world country which could not "afford" to provide its senior citizens with health care. How dare he impose his politics in the classroom! He's preaching socialism, and the University should clamp down. That has no place at BYU.

On another day after October general conference and the missionary reunions, he wrote of a conversation he had with Elder Jones—Dale.

Yesterday, Dale Jones and I saw each other and had a great time. He's going to the University, so we don't get to see each other much. And of course, going to that "apostate institution," he's a Democrat. I said that I think Goldwater's statement "extremism in defense of liberty" is right

on. Dale said, "1964 au-
water, 1965 hot water,
1966, no water." I didn't
say anything. We'll see.

Since they didn't see each other
except at reunions, he only wrote about
Dale Jones at general conference time
when the missionary reunions took place.
In April 1965, Goldwater having lost the
election, they didn't discuss politics.
Caleb wrote that they talked about
mission experiences and discussed the
nature of eternal progression:

At one point in our
discussion, Dale quoted
Elder Talmage as
indicating that people
could progress eternally,
even from the Telestial
Kingdom to the Terrestrial
Kingdom and from the
Terrestrial Kingdom to the
Celestial Kingdom. I said
that Elder McConkie wrote
that such teaching was
false, quoting a passage

stating that they could not
come where the Father
was, "worlds without end."

I don't know what
the answer is. Elder
McConkie seems quite
definite in his opinion. He
even goes so far as to say
that such teaching is
apostate. That's awfully
strong, especially when
others of the Brethren have
written and said such
things. It seems that
Heavenly Father would be
more loving if He allows
progression. I like Dale's
take more.

A journal entry written on a
Sunday afternoon in late February showed
further softening of boundaries.

I taught one of the
Gospel Doctrine classes
today. The subject was the

resurrection and the three degrees of glory. I had prepared a question or two for different places in the lesson manual to get deeper into the material. I asked, 'How does God's being a loving Father match his placing some of his children in lower kingdoms?'

Well, I got three quick answers. One elder said that men have agency. Another said that God must obey eternal laws. The third comment was God is righteous.

Then I read a passage from Elder James E. Talmage's *Articles of Faith*, pages 420-421, suggesting that eternal progression is for everyone and could even extend from kingdom to kingdom.

After class one of the RM's who responded to my question gave me the silent treatment. Another brother who hadn't commented came up to me and said, "I hope that idea is true. I love my dad, but he isn't celestial kingdom material. If he can progress eternally and advance to the Celestial Kingdom, then he can be with mom and we can all be together eternally."

And I remember the Prophet Joseph's saying that "truth tastes good."

11
"Teach and Learn"

During Caleb's last semester at
BYU, he wrote an entry in his journal
revealing his immediate future. One can
almost hear his shout of relief and
excitement upon getting a contract to
teach English at Paraganse Valley High
School.

One summer when
I was a child, we went to
Bryce Canyon National
Park, and we drove
through Paraganse Valley.
I thought at the time how
wonderful it would be to
live in one of the small
towns there. We'd have a
pasture with a couple of
horses, some beef steers
and perhaps some sheep.
It'd be so fun. I never
thought I'd get the chance

216

to live in such an idyllic
setting. Now I'm going!

He moved in August to Paraganse.
Though he had originally thought he
would teach high school age students, the
school included grades seven through
twelve, and as the new teacher, he was
assigned grades seven and eight. He
taught two English classes for each grade
and a remedial language arts class for
students in 7th through 9th grades. He
supervised a study hall one period and
had a free period for preparation in the
early afternoon, during which the
principal often assigned him to patrol the
hallways and the school grounds behind
the gym looking for students skipping
class.

Seventh graders began the school
year somewhat intimidated by being in
the large school, having lockers, changing
classrooms every period, and coming into
contact with older students in the
hallways. They were usually quiet and
silent in class. One morning in the third
week of class, this aura of peaceful

217

quiescence disappeared in first period with SueEllen Jenson's question, "My mom says you're not married. How come?"

"Your mom's right; I'm not married."

"How come?" came three responses.

"I don't know. I guess I just haven't met the right one yet."

Elsa Beth Petersen raised her hand and said, "You could marry Miss Olsen in Home Ec."

"We are here to learn English, not discuss Mr. Reynolds' personal life." He remembered to avoid using his first name so as to promote a proper distance between himself and the students. He tried to get the class focused on English grammar, "Your assignment for Wednesday is to examine the first three paragraphs of *To Kill a Mockingbird*. For each sentence write down the subject or subjects and the verbs going with each subject. Let's talk about the assignment. How can you identify the subject of a sentence?"

Silence. He sensed the unanswered question was distracting some students. He remembered being told by one supervising teacher while at the "Y" that silence is awkward for the students as well as for the teacher. "If you give in to the impulse to fill in the silence, your words will remove the awkwardness the students feel, let them off the hook. Don't do it. Just out wait them."

More silence. Finally, one of the girls raised her hand. When Caleb called on her, she said, "The subject of a sentence is what it's about."

"Thank you, Joanne. Will someone say what is the subject of the first sentence in the reading?"

Silence. The shy boy who sat on the side of the room next to the windows volunteered, "Jem?"

"Kissin' up already, Nate?" jeered one of the boys at the back of the room.

Another joined in, "Mr. Reynolds isn't interested" which reminded other students of the unanswered, "Why not?"

"Yeah, he can date Miss Olsen."

"Or go over to Panguitch," added still another.

"Okay, okay, guys. Cut it out. Respect everyone in the class. Thank you, Nate."

"Thank you, Nate," mocked two guys, and some girls tittered.

"Beth, would you please read the first sentence of the dialogue?"

"When he was nearly thirteen, my brother Jem got his arm badly broken at the elbow."

"What is the verb which goes with Jem in the first sentence? John?"

220

"Who cares?" John answered. "I don't."

A couple of others murmured their agreement.

Caleb was surprised at the indifference of class members and the hostility expressed by John. *I don't know where I'm going—and I'm getting there fast,* he thought. "Kathryn, can you help the class out? What is the verb in this first sentence?"

"I go by Kathy," she answered. "Yeah. I think the verb's *was.*"

"You're correct. *Was* is a verb going with the word *he.* What is the verb which goes with *Jem*?"

More silence. Finally, Nate ventured again, "*Got.*"

The class dragged on. Near the end of class, Caleb realized the grammar lesson wasn't going well. He decided he would just have them read the story. "I want you to read the first chapter of *To Kill A Mockingbird* in your text book by Friday. In the meantime, we will discuss what the story is about."

Tuesday, Wednesday and Thursday were no better. Some students read portions of the chapter, but they didn't say much in class. It appeared to Caleb that only two students continued reading to the end of the chapter.

"Who are the characters you have met in the story?" Caleb asked at the beginning of class on Friday.

Joanne said, "Jem and, oh, what's his name."

Beth added, "Dill."

"Who tells the story?" Caleb asked.

Nathan said, "We don't know. He hasn't told us."

"Is that true?" Caleb asked.

222

Silence followed.

"Hey, Nate, you blowin' your reputation. Teach'll pay no attention to you."

"Yeah," piped in another, "he'll go to Panguitch instead this weekend,"

"Well, Joe," Caleb spoke to one of the boys. "Who is telling the story?"

"Dunno."

"Well, check out page seven where they first meet Dill. What does Jem say?"

"He calls him 'Scout,' but she's a girl?"

"Yeah. What'd you expect. Boys don't talk like her, 'cept maybe Natie boy."

Ignoring the slur at Nathan, Caleb said, "For Monday, write two paragraphs explaining who Boo and Calpurnia are.

I'll call for the writing at the beginning of class."

Class hours seemed to go by fast, but days and weeks dragged on. Veterans' Day brought brief relief, but the holiday didn't prevent Tuesday from dawning as usual. Caleb could barely wait for Thanksgiving. School ended at noon on Wednesday, and Caleb drove out of town immediately after. It took him five hours to drive to Draper, counting time spent in Panguitch for a hamburger and malt.

By Christmas vacation, Caleb knew what he would do during the break. In the days after Christmas, he went to the various district offices in the Salt Lake Valley to apply for a job. He asked if the applications would be considered for more than one year in case there were not any vacancies and was told he would need to write to the districts each year if he were still interested. He even went north to Davis County School District and south to Alpine School District offices. As December edged toward the new year and the inevitable beginning of school, his

224

dread of returning to Paraganse Valley grew.

In English classes he had taken at the "Y," he had heard of epiphanies; he had read them in fiction works the classes had studied. But then, on December 30th, he experienced his own.

He returned with a lighter heart to Paraganse Valley. He prepared the course outlines for his upcoming classes. He reread the literature they would read in class and wrote down questions he could use in class discussions. He planned on alternative things he could lecture about should the students not have anything to say about the literature. He wrote a letter resigning his position effective June1st and mailed it to the district office in Panguitch.

The students were the same students he taught during fall term. They retained their indifference toward school, their unwillingness to discuss the literature, and for some, their hostility.

Most things didn't change, but for Caleb, it was totally different.

As May progressed, Caleb still did not know what he would do, only that that didn't matter. After classes ended, he submitted the grades and cleared out his office. He moved his belongings from his rental apartment and packed them into his car. He drove out of town and up the highway out of the valley without any joyous celebration, only contentment. He didn't know what would happen, only that it would, and everything would be okay.

He got a night watchman position with a steel fabricating company on the west side of Salt Lake City beside the D&RGW mainline to Denver. He timed one of his circuits through the yards of the company to watch the early morning passenger train for Denver and Chicago; he enjoyed trains, but especially this one—this train signaled his shift was almost over.

After a month and a half attending his parents' ward, immediately following

226

his twelve-hour shift on Saturday nights, he relaxed for an hour or so, then went to bed on Sunday mornings. Living in Draper and working Friday and Saturday nights, his social life shrank to Sunday afternoon drives after he woke up and to outings to some clubs in Salt Lake City where he met a few people he liked who accepted his drinking ginger ale, cranberry juice or Sprite.

He worked as a substitute teacher in Salt Lake City, Granite and Jordan School Districts when called, if he could fit it into his schedule. He resubmitted applications for teaching positions every spring.

Substitute teaching provided experience and some resumé filler. Substituting in junior high schools in Salt Lake Valley heightened his appreciation of those teachers who relished teaching junior high. On one occasion, some seventh-grade students answered the roll call with other students' names and they sat at different desks so the seating chart would not help him. He spent the hour asking students to stop talking loudly and to sit down in their chairs.

One girl said, "What'll you do, report us to our regular teacher? You don't know who I am."

By the end of the day, Caleb said, "I've never worked harder or been paid so much for accomplishing nothing. At least, they didn't bomb the school." After that day, he turned down requests to teach junior high.

Eventually he began to think of entering graduate school to work on a masters' degree. He filled out an application and submitted it to BYU and was accepted for the fall of 1978 to work on a masters in English literature.

12
"Belle"

As a new graduate teaching assistant, Caleb got to know Belle who, like Caleb, had returned for graduate work a few years after graduating from BYU. She recognized him from undergraduate classes, but he didn't remember her. He and Belle began spending time together out of their offices, going to meals, concerts, an occasional play.

When he discovered who her father was—one of the general authorities of the Church—he decided he would not be acceptable to her family, and he stopped seeing her except in the office suite. That might have been the end of the story had not Millie, another TA, asked him, "What's happened between you and Belle?"

"Oh, you know who her father is, don't you?"

"Yes, so what?" Millie asked,

"Well, I'm not anybody."

"That's crazy. I've been in their home several times, I go there for long weekends since I can't fly home. I'm going again for Thanksgiving. Brother Madsen's a fun guy, a bright mind, a good sense of humor."

Caleb started seeing Belle again.

On Monday after Thanksgiving, Belle told Caleb that she wanted her family to meet him. She suggested the second Friday of December for dinner at their place in the Avenues of Salt Lake City. Caleb accepted her invitation.

After Christmas vacation, they went on a Saturday night to *Romeo and Juliet* at the Fine Arts Center on campus. Even though the actors were all students, Caleb was thrilled with Romeo's words in the balcony scene. He choked up, stifling a sob, at the final scene when Romeo drinks the poison brought from Mantua.

230

Afterwards in his car, Caleb was quiet while driving to Belle's apartment, sifting through the emotions of the play. *Romeo's words are so poetic. How deeply he loves. It's so sad.* They sat briefly in the car, she commenting on the quality of the performance, he remembering the scenes of the play, the poetry, saying nothing. He then got out of the car, opened her door, and walked her to her apartment. There he said "goodnight," and walked back to his car.

One night at the end of a date, they sat talking casually about something, when a mini competition emerged over a medallion on a necklace. Belle tucked the medallion inside her blouse, daring Caleb to retrieve it. He did. And in the tug of war, he broke the necklace chain. His triumph in obtaining the medallion was tempered by his embarrassment at having broken her necklace. He immediately apologized and handed her the medallion. An awkward short silence followed, then he walked her to her apartment door, kissed her softly and returned home. Only months later did he realize that probably she had tucked the medallion into her blouse as invitation, not competition.

Having heard comments from the guys over the years about their dates and what many did beyond the official activity of the date, Caleb had some concerns about marriage, particularly as he and various girlfriends progressed beyond the early dating stage. This experience with Belle was no different. They continued dating over months. Eventually, in early 1980, he sought counsel from the only authority he knew of, the bishop of his student ward. Once in his office, however, he didn't know how to begin. They performed the usual "dance" of talking about the weather, upcoming ward events, the current BYU basketball fortunes.

"Bishop," Caleb finally began, "I don't know how to say this, but I'm attracted to other men."

"Have you had any sexual contact with any other man?" the bishop asked.

"No, no." Then after a pause, "but I find many men. . . attractive."

"What do you think about when you see an attractive man? Do you imagine sex with him?"

"No. . . . I don't know what I would do, how we would have sex. I would kiss him—on the lips."

"Have you masturbated with another man?"

"No," Caleb answered.

"Are you dating women?"

"Yes, I guess. I've been dating another graduate assistant in English. But I'm not sexually attracted to her. . . . Or to any other woman."

"Well, Caleb, I can promise you that if you refrain from sexual activity with other men, and if you continue dating and get married to a woman in the temple, the Lord will heal you. You will

233

be cured of these attractions. You have been diligent in the past, and the Lord will not desert you."

"Do I tell Belle about my...."

"No. The Lord will heal you and take these feelings away. She does not need to know.

Caleb remembered how the bishop of his home ward had told him that if he was successful as a missionary, he would be healed, he would no longer feel attracted to men. He was a successful missionary, but his 'problem' did not disappear. He still found himself attracted to men. He dated women because he knew he should get married. He enjoyed their company but felt no sexual desire towards them.

Several days after his discussion with the bishop, Caleb entered a men's restroom in Campus Center. As he was washing his hands, he glanced into the mirror. In the reflection, he could see

through the crack between the door and
the wall of a stall a man masturbating.

*Oh, I want to be in there with him!
O, Lord, I'm so evil! How can I be
forgiven? I'm turning "like a dog to its
vomit."* He fasted and prayed the next day
for faith. He returned to the bishop for
help and again received the same promise
the bishop had given him earlier. The
bishop also encouraged him to check in
with him regularly. Caleb did so.

Despite his attraction to other men
and his lack of any sexual attraction to
Belle, he asked Belle to marry him. They
set a date in July 1980. Belle's father
married them in the Salt Lake Temple.

13
"Wedding, Honeymoon"

For their honeymoon, Caleb reserved a room for three nights at The Inn at Snowbird in Little Cottonwood Canyon above Salt Lake City.

The reception began at 7:00 PM the night after the temple ceremony. As usual with wedding receptions, many guests stayed and talked after greeting the bride and groom, their families, and the attendants. The formal reception line took a break at 8:30 PM for the cake cutting, followed by more casual group visits. The line reassembled for later arriving guests, and by 10:00, Belle and Caleb had greeted all the late-arriving guests.

Belle changed out of her wedding gown, and just prior to their departure, she tossed her bouquet to the crowd gathered for the final sendoff. Caleb and Belle were immediately on their way, driving the forty minutes to Snowbird near the top of the canyon.

They reached Snowbird tired, or more accurately, exhausted. After checking in, Caleb and a valet carried all the luggage to their room. Even as tired as he was, Caleb remembered to give the valet a tip. When Belle heard him close the door, she called out, "I'm in the bathroom getting ready. I'll be out in five minutes."

Caleb stood in the middle of the room. *Now what?* Suddenly he turned, opened his suitcase and grabbed the new pair of pajamas he had previously packed on top of everything else. He put them down, untied his bow tie, removed his tuxedo coat, laid it down and started to take of his pants.

Then he realized he had to remove his shoes first. He sat down on the floor where he was, untied his shoes and set them on the floor beside the closet door. Standing up, he removed his trousers, hung them up and looked for the coat to hang it with the trousers.

He picked up his pajamas again, but had to lay them down to take his shirt off. The cuff links he received from his father, CT, had two jeweled ends connected by a chain, not easy to remove, or put on.

Hurry, he thought.

"Finally," he whispered, after getting the second cuff link out. Crossing the room to a dresser, he dropped the cufflinks on it and then removed the studs from his shirt front—also frustratingly difficult.

Come on, come on!... At last! he thought when he succeeded in removing the last stud. He began taking off his shirt as he walked back to the closet.

He hung the shirt up and grabbed his pajamas. He began to put on the bottoms, lost his balance and moved to the bed to sit down to put them on. He shivered, pulled on the bottoms and slipped his arms into the pajama top. He shivered so badly he had difficulty buttoning the pajama top.

Belle came out of the bathroom and crossed toward the bed.

"Finally!" she said and sat beside him.

"Why! you're shaking. Are you okay?" she asked.

He shivered more violently. "I don't know, I guess, maybe not."

"Let's get you under the covers." He stood up, they pulled the sheets down, and he lay down on the bed. Belle retrieved a thin blanket, wrapped it around him, and lay down beside him, holding him in her arms. Gradually his shivering subsided. Lying there, exhausted, they fell asleep, spooning.

On the next day, Belle and Caleb rode the tram up to Hidden Peak. From the top of the tram ride, several ski runs and hiking trails were available, including ways to walk back down to the base. Caleb had talked to the concierge in the Inn before leaving for the tram and decided that they should ride the tram both ways and do a shorter, easier hike once they returned. They chose to take the Chauner's Loop trail. On the hike, they met a family of five, two teenage boys, a nine-year old girl, and the parents, Bob and Kathy. Both families had brought a lunch with them, so they shared a picnic.

With Bob and Caleb soon talking about sports, work, careers, Kathy asked Belle, "Tell me about your wedding. Where were you married?"

"Dad married us in the Salt Lake Temple yesterday morning. My parents, brothers and their wives, and my sister and her husband were there. Caleb's older sister and his parents were there. Some aunts and uncles also attended. I think many of my extended family were relieved I was finally getting married."

"If I understand correctly, only a few people attend the actual temple wedding. Did you have a larger reception afterwards? What was the it like?"

"Oh, we had a beautiful reception last night. We were able to schedule one of the ballrooms at the Hotel Utah, right downtown. The reception line was at one end of the ballroom and at the other end, a small group of friends formed an orchestra to play dance music so everyone could dance. In between the dancing and the reception line we had tables set up for light refreshments."

"What did you serve?"

"A caterer provided light refreshments. Cold cuts, veggies, cheeses, crackers and dips, cookies, pastries, and fruit juices."

"What colors did you choose?"

"My dress was floor length with light lavender, and blue accents. The veil was studded with baroque pearls which I love. My bouquet was primarily lavender roses, phlox, purple waxflower, and one white rose tied up with a blue ribbon. The bridesmaids wore light lilac dresses with silver grey sashes and blue-ribbon trim on the necklines and sleeves. My sister was matron of honor; she wore a lilac dress with a white sash."

"I like the blue and white accents. They must have been really beautiful," Kathy said.

"Oh, they were. Thank you."

"So, you came up this morning?"

"No, we came up last night after the reception."

"Wow," Kathy said. "Did you have room service for a late breakfast?"

"No, we've already ridden the tram up to the top and back. . ."

"Really. We didn't leave our room until...." Kathy paused.

242

Turning to Caleb, Belle said, "Honey, I'm quite tired. Can we go back soon?"

Caleb consulted the map he got from the concierge. "I think just a little bit ahead, this trail crosses another trail that goes directly down to the lodges. We can take that, though it may be steeper."

When the two couples reached the trail junction, the boys were far ahead. Belle and Caleb turned right toward Snowbird village while Bob, Kathy, and their daughter continued along the Chauner's Loop Trail.

"Would you like some ice cream?" Caleb asked as they walked across the floor of the canyon toward their room.

"That sounds really good," Belle answered. "But I don't want to sit down. I just want to go up to the room. Just get me a cone, please."

"Sure. What flavor do you want?"

"If it's Snelgrove's, Rocky Road. If it's not Snelgrove's, get me vanilla."

They ate their cones of Rocky Road ice cream in the lobby of the Inn and on the elevator, and then, after removing their hiking clothes, washing their faces and brushing their teeth, they lay down on the bed, holding each other and fell asleep.

Next morning, Belle awoke fairly early. As Caleb was still asleep, she got up, showered, and dressed. She read for a while, then woke Caleb asking if he wanted breakfast. He quickly got up, showered and shaved, then they went down to a restaurant for breakfast.

After eating, they walked around the various shops in the different lodges. Belle wanted to look for some nice gifts for her bridesmaids and matron of honor. Caleb wanted to see what Belle particularly liked so he could buy her a gift. When she went to the ladies' room during their window shopping, he returned to the jewelry store to purchase a

244

necklace she had liked, had it boxed and gift wrapped, and tucked the box into the pocket of a light jacket he was carrying.

Having eaten a rather hearty but late breakfast they weren't hungry until mid-afternoon. Because Caleb had made a reservation for them for dinner at the Lodge Bistro, they snacked on two appetizers from one of the more casual restaurants. Belle had decided on the gifts for her bridesmaids, so they returned to the jewelry store to purchase them. After Caleb settled the bill at the jewelry store, they took the elevator to their room where they changed into dressier clothes for dinner.

Dinner was delicious. After the waiter cleared the plates and they had selected their desserts, Caleb gave the gift-wrapped package to Belle.

"Oh, Caleb. This is so beautiful. Thank you."

Caleb rose and went behind her to fasten the necklace clasp. He kissed her on her head.

"I'm glad you like it," he said.

After dinner, they went back to their room and prepared for bed. That night, Caleb consummated their marriage. Afterwards, Caleb lay still beside Belle, hoping to hear from her breathing that she slept.

Is she asleep yet? I can't tell. Dear Father, this has got to get better. I don't know what to do. It seems so difficult; so unpleasant to me. It's so. . . so contrary, to me. God, please help me. Carefully so as not to awaken Belle, he rolled over facing away from her. He fell asleep.

The next morning, they checked out of the lodging and began the drive back down the canyon to the Salt Lake Valley. They didn't stop in the city to see her parents nor in Draper to see his; they just drove back to Provo.

246

14
"Interlude: Fall Semester"

Three nights after Caleb and Belle returned to Provo, he again had sex with Belle. Afterwards, as they lay silently beside each other, he noticed she was weeping quietly.

Oh, Father, he prayed silently, *I'm failing her. I hate hurting her, but I dislike having sex with her. It's so unpleasant. So wrong. What can I do?* He received no answer; he felt no confirmation.

As time passed, he continued trying to have sex with Belle, but sex soon happened only when she hinted at it with her actions or when she requested it directly. As both Caleb and Belle were busy with classes and teaching, Belle didn't approach Caleb for sex often.

Caleb tried to keep their social life, their dating life, going at least. He

247

got tickets to a Shakespeare play in late October. They also went to most of the home football games that fall, frequently meeting up with his parents after the games when he knew they would be coming from Draper. In November, Belle told him that *Porgy and Bess*, with a Black traveling cast, would be presented at Kingsbury Hall on the University of Utah campus in late January and February. They decided to get tickets to *Porgy and Bess* for February after they had submitted grades for their students.

They were now members of a married students ward. Their ward did a food drive for poor families in Provo in early December and then had Christmas party before the break.

They spent Thanksgiving weekend with both extended families. They stayed two nights in Draper and one night in Salt Lake City. Then realizing they needed to correct papers, they returned Saturday morning to Provo. During the Christmas break they visited Temple Square and downtown Salt Lake City to see the lights, but spent most of those days writing their own papers and correcting student work. January was filled with grading student papers, preparing tests, writing their papers, and finally studying and taking final exams.

15
"Revelations"

Chemistry. Electricity. These filled Kingsbury as *Porgy and Bess* moved through Act I. A tall, muscular, beautiful man played Crown. Equally svelte, Bess radiated her attraction to him, in spite of her loving Porgy. Feeling himself more similar to quiet Porgy than to Crown, Caleb glanced at Belle near the end of that scene. Belle glowed, her eyes fixed upon the stage.

I can never be Crown. Belle can love me, but I'm only Porgy, Ultimately... Ultimately she will have to sacrifice much of what she wishes for, wants and deserves, to stay with me. As he mulled over these thoughts, he realized, *I want Crown just as much as Bess—or Belle—wants him. I want a man, strong and beautiful.* Sorrow flowed through him.

250

The promises had not been
fulfilled. He had kept all the
conditions—an honorable mission,
courtship, temple marriage,
consummating that marriage, participating
in the Church, living honorably and
chastely.

I still crave contact with men; I
have no more physical, sexual interest in
Belle—or any other woman—than I have
ever had.

For the next four weeks, Caleb
mulled over his relation to Belle.
Repeatedly trying to disprove his
realization at *Porgy and Bess*, Caleb
saddened. Later in the semester, writing
papers for his classes and grading student
papers dragged him down further.

"Something's the matter. What is
it," Belle finally asked one evening.

"Nothing."

After a short silence, Belle said, "Something's bothering you. You're silent, sullen at times. We. . ."

"There's nothing the matter!"

Within the hour, Caleb offered, "I'm sorry I snapped at you. It is not your fault. Please forgive me."

"Please tell me what's bothering you."

"I can't, at least not yet. Maybe later. Go to bed. I'm staying up to do some writing."

Belle awoke at 3:15, found Caleb's side of the bed empty, and saw him asleep on the sofa in the living room.

She covered him with a flannel sheet. She wanted to go back to sleep, but as she walked back to bed, she couldn't help thinking, *Where have I failed? Have I been too sloppy with the housekeeping? Have I become unattractive? Have I put too much emphasis on my own classes*

and teaching? Am I not cooking well
enough? Am I not even cooking often
enough? Have I gained weight? Does he
not find me attractive?

The following Sunday morning
just prior to leaving for church, Caleb
said, "I need to talk with dad. After
dinner, I'm driving up to Draper. If you
wish to visit your family, you can drop me
off and take the car on into Salt Lake. I'll
telephone you at your father's when I'm
ready to go."

"Are you going to discuss this
problem with . . ." she paused,
remembering his anger. "Why couldn't I
just go to Draper with you?"

"I need to spend some time alone
with dad. No mom, no you; dad and me
alone. Maybe later, I'll tell you."

Belle opted to stay at home in
their apartment in Provo. Caleb got into
the car and drove to Draper via the
freeway leading to Salt Lake City,
arriving at the family home about 3:00

PM. CT and Emma had finished dinner; and they had washed the dishes and were sitting in the living room, each reading in silence. The sound of a car entering the driveway on the far side of the house caused them to look up at each other, questioning. CT got up, walked into the dining room to look out the window when Caleb opened the kitchen door.

"Knock, knock. Anyone home?" he asked as he entered.

"Caleb! It's good to see you. Something the matter?" CT asked, walking toward Caleb.

"No. Just wanted to see you for a bit. Hi, mom," he greeted Emma as she walked into the kitchen from the dining room.

"Caleb. It's so good to see you. Where's Belle?" she asked.

"Belle decided not to come. She has papers to grade," Caleb said, knowing this could not be the real answer as Belle

254

would not be grading papers on Sunday. "I offered her the chance to drive on in to Salt Lake to visit her folks, but she decided to stay at home."

"Why didn't she want to visit with us?" CT questioned.

"Oh, it's not that. I told her I was coming to see dad, that I needed to have some time without anyone else. Sorry mom, but this is just dad and me."

"I no longer keep secrets from your mother," CT asserted.

"You won't have to for long." Then after a pause, "Let's sit down for a spell first and catch up."

"Well, come into the living room." Emma said turning back toward the dining room and its connection through the front hall to the living room. CT and Caleb followed her. "I was reading *Middlemarch*."

"How far into it are you?"

"Not far; far enough to see that Dorothea is quite smitten with Mr. Casaubon. I think that's his name. Does she remain so worshipful?"

"Oh, I think you'll come to admire her. But, yes, she is a bit worshipful, isn't she?" Turning to CT, Caleb asked, "What have you been doing today?"

"Well, after the priesthood lesson was so disappointing, I decided to explore the subject beyond the manual. Sure, it asks some appropriate questions, but it offers simple answers, and the instructor never goes beyond the manual. There are so many questions available on the topic, and I, for one, would like to explore those questions. As it is, priesthood meeting is so boring, I wish I could skip it."

"Tch, tch, tch," Caleb teased. "You're getting to be a bad as me."

"As bad as I," Emma inserted. "You're an English major. Haven't they helped me teach you grammar?"

"Oh, mom. We no longer speak as the 'Victorians' did in the early part of the century. Dictionaries and grammars are now more descriptive of the language rather than the old-fashioned prescriptive approach. And yes, there are still some standards," he added before Emma could argue her usual response.

A little later, Caleb said, "Dad, please come with me for a ride."

"Really," Emma inserted. "I can give you some privacy. Don't you trust your mother?"

"That isn't the reason. I trust you," Caleb answered. "I just want us to be uninterrupted and able to focus on topic."

Caleb and CT left through the kitchen back door and got into Caleb's car. He backed out of the driveway and drove north to the road stretching from the main part of town east to the mountains. Caleb turned right and followed the road until the pavement ended at the last houses and then continued on the dirt road, turning south and climbing the side of the mountain to the bench created by ancient Lake Bonneville. At one of the wide spots in the road, Caleb turned the car west to face the valley and stopped.

"Dad, I've stewed over this for weeks and still do not know how to say what I want to tell you."

"Caleb, I'm afraid I don't want to hear this, but... Please, go on. It has to be important, so tell me what's on your mind."

"I feel disconnected. I'm afraid you and mom, and Ellie, Maryelle, won't love me when you hear what I have to say."

"Caleb, we will love you. We may not always agree with what you do and how you feel, but we love you."

"I've come to realize that I need Belle to divorce me."

258

"Why? You aren't having an affair with another woman, are you?" CT asked, sure that Caleb was innocent of that.

"No, I'm not having an affair with anyone. I. . . I don't love her. Yes, I do, but not that way. I can't give her what she needs and wants and deserves. I don't love women; I don't imagine having sex with a woman. When Belle and I have sex, it's fake. It's torture."

"Caleb," CT began then paused. "Caleb, I know... I know how difficult this is. You can make it anyway, in the marriage, I mean. As you may know, your mother and I are not very. . . not very. . . Stop and think. Maryelle is seven years older than you. Emma wanted a son, begged me for a son."

"Did you ever fall in love?"

"Yes. Do you mean with your mother? Yes, I love your mother, but. . ."

"Did you ever fall in love, romantically, feeling sexually attracted to another?"

"Yes, I did. . . But we never acted upon our, or at least my desire."

"Would you tell me about this love?"

"I. . ." CT paused. "I've never said a word of this to anyone. I don't know if I. . . ."

"That's okay. Maybe sometime in the future." Then after a pause, "Why did you marry mom?"

"I moved to Draper with my father. Sometime later, Emma visited Aunt Mary and Uncle Brigham and came to church on that Sunday. I just knew when I first saw her that I would marry her. So, I courted her and married her. We've had a fairly good life. That's how I know you can make your marriage work."

"I cannot love a woman the way she deserves, the way I deserve. It's too lonely. Marriage to Belle leaves me more isolated than when I was single. I cannot get close to any man at church or in school out of fear that it may go too far or that he may feel I'm sexually attracted and be offended. I have women friends, but they don't—they can't—fulfill my social, my emotional need."

"I don't seem to understand why you feel this need. I understand—I know loneliness, but it's just something you learn to live with."

"It's too big a hollow for me. I admire you for preserving your marriage and family. I am grateful for you in our lives, but I cannot live this loneliness." After a pause, Caleb added, "Anyway, I wanted you to know. I'll probably ask Belle for a divorce—or an annulment—come summer. Then I think I have to go to the 'U' to finish my degree; I don't know about that yet. I want to make the situation as easy for both of us as I can." I got here!

"I guess you aren't asking for my approval on this; I don't approve. But, Caleb, you are my son. I will always love you, and you are always welcome in our home. I will give you a father's blessing if you want one."

Caleb reached across the car seat and hugged his father. CT kissed him on his cheek. Both men cried. "Will you give me a blessing for guidance here, now, in the car?"

CT placed his hands upon Caleb's head. "In the name of Jesus Christ and by the power of the Melchizedek Priesthood, I bless you in this time of trial. I bless you that the Lord will send his spirit to guide you, so you will know what steps you should take. I bless you with peace in your heart as you follow the spirit's guidance. I bless you to listen carefully to the words of the prophets in your seeking God's guidance. I bless you that regardless of your decisions, you will know we love you and want you in our lives. In the name of Jesus Christ, Amen."

On the way back down to the valley, Caleb asked, "What will you tell mom?"

"That's a good question. What do you want me to tell her? What do you want me to not tell her?"

"I want to tell her, but I'm not ready to tell her about Belle and me tonight. Tell her I'm thinking of transferring to the 'U.' Don't tell her anything else. Maybe I'll come up during the week somehow and tell her about Belle and me. I should tell Belle before I talk to mom, so I don't know if I can do that this week. I don't know when I'll talk to Belle or to mom. I don't know."

Caleb drove into the driveway. "I'm not coming in. Please tell mom I need to get back to Provo."

CT got out of the car and watched as Caleb backed out of the driveway and drove away.

263

16
"Talking About 'It'"

There is never a good time to broach difficult topics. Caleb tried to find such a time, but Belle also needed to know what was bothering him, so eventually she asked him again. Caleb told her he was gay. He asked her to divorce him and get a temple annulment of their marriage, and two days later, he moved out of the apartment.

The day after telling Belle to seek an annulment, Caleb went back to Draper.

No, no, no. No! O, God, don't do this to me, Emma thought. But she said nothing.

Caleb waited in silence for a minute. "I've told Belle, and I'm moving in with a friend for the time being. If I stay at the 'Y,' I'll find a place for next fall, probably with some other men students."

264

"Why not continue in your marriage?" Emma finally asked.

"It won't work. It isn't a marriage."

"Well do something. Make it a marriage."

"Mom, I'm gay, a homosexual. I can't..."

"The prophets have said there's no such thing as a homosexual. You have to keep trying. The Lord will heal you."

"It doesn't work that way. I am homosexual. Nothing will change that. He doesn't change me. I've tried over and over. The promises aren't true. They don't work," Caleb responded.

After Caleb left to return to Provo, Emma confronted CT.

"How long have you known about this?"

"About two weeks. When he came up that Sunday afternoon and took me for a ride."

"Why didn't you tell me? Why didn't you stop him?"

"He told me he wanted to tell you himself. He said he wasn't ready to tell you that day."

"And you agreed with that? How could you? What in heaven's name is wrong with you?"

"I asked him to reconsider. I told him I disagreed with his decision. I also told him I love him and he would always be welcome in my home. He is our son."

"Yes, I love him too. That's why this hurts me so much. He's making a huge mistake."

"Maybe so, I don't know. He's thought about this for months. While it's not what I'd wish him to do—and I said so when he told me—I need to respect his decision. This is his home. I won't make his decision the basis of my accepting him, loving him, supporting him."

"I don't want to lose Belle," Emma said.

"We don't have a lot to do with that. If Caleb and Belle remain friends, we can continue to include her in some family gatherings. But we cannot really welcome her if our purpose is to get them back together. That mustn't be our role."

"Well, if not ours, whose role is it?"

"Theirs. Theirs and theirs alone. Our role is to love them and support their decision."

Caleb's announcement that he was gay knifed Emma into her core being. *How did I fail as a mother so he became gay? What have I done? Did I mother him too much? Did I prevent CT and him from bonding?*

Emma's dialogue with God over the ensuing weeks continued in much the same vein as her words to CT on the day Caleb told her he was gay. Gradually, though, she modified her prayer to have an opportunity to welcome Belle back into their home and then shortly afterwards to seek help in understanding Caleb.

Discussion of Caleb's being gay also took place between Caleb and Belle. About a month after Caleb moved out of the apartment he and Belle had shared, he came back to retrieve clothes and books he needed. Although they had talked briefly about his being gay, this was the first time they talked in-depth about that.

"Why? Why do we need to separate?" Belle asked Caleb.

"Belle, I don't know what to say. I can't really function with you as a husband."

"How do you know. We've only been together for a few months."

268

"Have you been satisfied with our relationship? I haven't. But I can't do. . . . I can't function as a husband."

"Shouldn't we try to talk through what's bothering you. What am I doing wrong? What can I do to help?"

"Nothing. You're not doing anything wrong. I'm sorry, but there's nothing you can do."

"If it's so final; if you've made your choice, why didn't you talk to me—no, tell me plainly—before we married?"

"Belle, I didn't want to say this, but you've asked. I was instructed by priesthood leaders not to tell you anything. They promised if I married you, everything would work out. You wouldn't ever need to know."

"Well, let's work at it."

"What is there to work at? I'm attracted to men, not women. I've

269

'worked' at it for years. None of the promises made me by bishops and other priesthood leaders has been fulfilled."

"What do you mean, you've worked at it for years?"

"I first recognized that my attraction to men, to other boys, was different from most boys, when I was fourteen. I know now that I've always been interested in other boys. But at fourteen, I confessed to the bishop of my ward that I was attracted to other boys, sexually attracted to them, not just as friends. He told me that if I would avoid any actions with other boys, if I dated girls, if I honored my priesthood, the Lord would cure me. I obeyed. I did what he said I should do.

"When it was time for a mission, I told the bishop I was attracted to other men. He promised me that if I kept myself clean, both in thoughts and actions, I could have a mission opportunity. If I filled an honorable mission I would be cured. I filled an honorable mission. My

270

companions and I had baptisms almost every month; that was wonderful at the time. I believed the gospel and bore firm testimony of it. I know many were touched by the spirit through my missionary work.

"No change. At the end of my mission, I was still sexually attracted to other elders, to men who were members of the Church in the cities where I was working, to teenagers who lived in the area. I had kept myself clean: I had not *done* anything, not *said* anything, nor approached anyone, but I still was entranced by men. *None* of the promised blessings occurred."

Caleb paused and thought, *This whole situation frustrates me. I'm arguing with Belle; I should be telling this to the bishop, not Belle. She hasn't broken any promises.*

"When I came home," Caleb resumed, "I received the same promises again: date women, get married, be faithful in my priesthood callings, and

God would change me. I've done all that for the three or four years before we met and for the months we've been dating."

He stopped again, then with a bitter edge to his voice, "I even obeyed the bishop's instructions that I not tell you of this problem. He said I should marry you and trust in the Lord's blessing. A lot of good that has done. You've been hurt, and I've been repeatedly deceived by priesthood leaders, or abandoned by God, I don't know which. Promises, promises, and more promises. There's been no fulfillment."

Oh, Father in Heaven, Belle thought. *He's become angry just talking about this. Please, I don't want to talk about this now. Oh, Father, help me. I don't want to hear him when he's so angry. Why? Why can't we talk rationally, temperately, about how to make him interested? I don't understand.*

A telephone call for Belle interrupted their conversation, and Caleb went into the bedroom to get items he

272

needed. He returned to the living room of the apartment as Belle finished her telephone conversation.

"I'm sorry for getting angry while we talked. I'm not angry with you; you're not to blame for our situation," Caleb said.

"I'm sorry to see you angry, especially with the Church."

"Well, with whom should I be angry?" he demanded.

"Maybe you shouldn't be angry with anyone."

"Well, I am. I'll leave it at that," he answered. "I'm going."

"I wish you would stay here where you belong, where we belong together."

"Oh, Belle. I'm sorry for the pain this is causing you. But we don't belong together. I can't. . . I cannot . . . be a husband to you."

"Doesn't our temple sealing contradict that statement? Can't the Lord help us make it work?"

"Whether or not He could isn't the point. He doesn't; that's all."

"If you'd give us more time, maybe I could become more attractive to you."

"Belle, honey, you are as attractive to me as any other woman, more so than most. It isn't that."

Shortly after, Caleb left.

17
"Dr. Louisa Belknap"

Three weeks of hell engulfed Belle after Caleb told her she should ask for a temple annulment of their marriage. Then Belle telephoned Dr. Louisa Belknap, an English professor at the "Y" whom she had admired for years.

"Dr. Belknap, I would like to make an appointment to talk to you. It's personal, not related to my degree, and it's quite important. I need help."

"Certainly, Belle," Professor Belknap said. "My normal office hours tomorrow end at 2:30. Can you come in then? We can spend whatever time you need, maybe even get supper together as well, depending upon your obligations."

"Thank you," Belle spoke with relief. "I'll come then."

During the following hours, Belle felt the whole range of emotions. *Why am I going to Dr. Belknap? She's obviously not my bishop; she's not my visiting teacher or my Relief Society President.*

But she's been so involved in women's issues on campus. She's called for equal pay for women. She's promoted concerns of women students.

But she isn't a marriage counselor or a psychologist. What can she do for me?

Perhaps she'll know where I can turn.

She's so busy with students, I shouldn't take up her time.

She offered to help. Quit stewing.

Maybe she felt she had to. A sense of obligation.

Belle experienced these thoughts over and over. The next afternoon, her

276

questions about her decision to turn to Dr. Belknap increased in intensity. Nevertheless, she went to the Jesse Knight Building, climbed the stairs to the third floor, and when she got to Dr. Belknap's office, she knocked on the door.

Dr. Belknap opened the door almost immediately. "Come in, come in. Sit down. How are you doing?"

"Well, I don't know," Belle answered hesitantly.

"First of all, are you comfortable talking here or do you wish to go elsewhere?"

"That's a good question. How secure, sound-proof, are the walls? Can I be open and have our conversation be private?" Belle asked.

"I'm quite sure the offices are sound-proof. I've never heard conversations between professors and students from either side or from across the hall. If you'd feel safer walking, however, I'm willing to do that."

"Well, for the time being, let's talk here then," Belle answered.

"Before going any further, tell me about your classes this semester. How are they? How are you doing on your thesis?"

Relieved to have something else to talk about, Belle started talking of her enjoyment of the language course she was taking.

"On the surface, history of English language seems like such a dry topic for a lit major. But I love it. I find the study of the grammar changes, the pronunciation variations and shifts exciting to know about. I already notice these insights help with my poetry writing."

"You're still writing then? Now that you're no longer in my writing classes, I don't get to see your work regularly."

278

"Well, I have been writing into this semester, but. ..."

Dr. Belknap waited in silence for Belle to continue.

"To be honest, my marriage is . . . maybe ... failing. Caleb asked me or told me about three weeks ago that I should ask the Church for an annulment of our temple marriage and . . . and file for divorce."

Belle began crying. Dr. Belknap handed her a box of Kleenex she had on her desk.

"What have you done since he said this?"

"Cried a lot." Belle answered.

"Have you talked to anyone? A marriage counselor? Your bishop? Your father?"

"No," Belle answered softly. "I didn't want to go to the bishop. I don't want to endanger either Caleb's or my standing with the University. We're both within a year and a half of finishing degrees. I don't know any marriage counselors or personal therapists to turn to. I knew that you have helped so many women and have advocated for women, so I decided to come to you."

"Thank you for the confidence. Rest assured, *no one,* not your bishop nor any other faculty or staff will hear any of this until you tell them. I will not.

"I'm only a first resource. I don't want to put you off; I hope you will continue to come to visit whenever you wish. I'm not trained, however, as a therapist nor as a marriage counselor. If you are willing, I will put you in touch with two women in Salt Lake City. One is a marriage counselor who has done really good work with women in various situations. The second woman is a psychiatrist with a specialty in sex therapy, not that you necessarily need that; I don't know.

280

"Both women are highly regarded professionally. They respect their clients' privacy rights and their clients' religious feelings, but neither would be recommended by LDS Social Services. I don't think the psychiatrist, the sex therapist, is even a member. I want you to know that beforehand. Social Services is also an alternative.

"Now I can be a listening ear personally and an advocate in any campus situation. So, let me begin with the listening. What has happened?"

"Well, I noticed tensions almost, no, even from the beginning. I just didn't know what was the matter. Caleb talked normally about other things, things other than our relationship. But he didn't say anything about us.

"We had awkward times with sex. We didn't have sex the first few nights of our honeymoon. When we finally did, it was . . . well . . . terrible." Belle began crying again. "I felt I had failed as a woman, as a Mormon woman, as a wife.

We tried a couple of times when I prodded, but, in hindsight, never by his initiative."

"Finally, he told me to file for divorce. A couple of days later, he explained that he's gay, homosexual . . . and that he cannot live with a woman."

Belle's sobs interrupted her words, and Dr. Belknap sat quiet, stunned. She reached out her hand and put it on Belle's shoulder.

"We need to get you in touch with one—or both—of these women in Salt Lake City. I'll telephone them, ask for the earliest opening they might have and get back in touch with you to see if you can make it. Then when we've got a date and time, I'll drive you up and introduce you. In the meantime, you decide if this is the right way for you to go, if you feel comfortable taking this path.

"I am not recommending seeking priesthood advice. You know I feel women are as entitled to revelation in

282

their personal lives as men are in theirs. Women are entitled —they do not need to consult with ward or stake leaders on many personal issues; they can go directly to the Lord and receive answers. But this is your decision, not mine. Regardless of how you choose to go, please feel welcome to come back here to talk."

"Thank you for listening. Yes, I'd like to go to Salt Lake City. In the meantime, over the next two or three days, I will try to discern the best way for me to act."

"Well, let's walk to my car, then go get some supper unless you're expected home to make supper for Caleb."

"No, no. Caleb is staying with a former roommate or at his parents' home in Draper. In essence, he's moved out," and she cried again.

"Well, then, let's go. You don't want to eat alone at home tonight, do you? After supper I'll take you to your apartment."

Three days later, Belle called Dr. Belknap in her office. "I'm still not sure what I should do. So, I'd like to meet the counselor but with her knowing I'm not certain if I should do more than just meet her. Do you think that would be okay with her? Or do I need to commit before I go the first time?"

"I'll telephone her this afternoon to lay out your feelings so she can decide. If she's willing, I'll make an appointment for as soon as you can go."

"Thank you. Can you call me . . . No. I'll call you tomorrow morning at your office. What time will you be in?" Belle asked.

"I have a class from 9:00 to 10:30 and will come to the office after that. When is a good day for you to travel with me to Salt Lake?"

"Friday afternoon is best for me. Next week Wednesday afternoon would be okay. My classes meet Tuesdays and Thursdays; I teach Monday, Wednesday, and Fridays in the morning."

"Good. I'll call her this afternoon after my teaching and get back to . . . Oh, wait, you wanted to call me? I can call you tonight."

"Yes, that will be okay. Even if Caleb comes back home today, there's no reason I should hide this from him."

The decision to go into counseling is never easy for a Mormon woman. *I'm not supposed to air my dirty laundry before outsiders,* Belle told herself. *If my marriage is failing, I have priesthood leaders whom I should consult. . . . But, then, my husband doesn't want this authority. He wants me to break it all off. My bishop is an accounting professor. What does he know about giving marriage advice?*

I don't want to go to Dad; he suggested I accept Caleb's proposal even though I wondered about his not seeming interested in physical contact with me.

I've already gone beyond what the Church would suggest as acceptable for a woman by turning to a woman professor. The acceptable ways all seem like dead ends.

But if I don't do things the way the Lord counsels, how can I expect right solutions? I never should have turned to Professor Belknap.

But I did . . . so maybe I should follow up. I don't have to commit to working with this woman. And if she demands a commitment upfront, I'll take that as inspiration that I should not seek her help further.

Everywhere Belle went, she debated with herself throughout the day. These thoughts interrupted her research hours in the library. They pervaded her grocery shopping on her way home. Then

286

as she cooked a supper, her thoughts changed. *Perhaps Dr. Belknap has forgotten. Oh, that's a relief. No. I need to face this. . . I need help to face this. If this avenue is not open, I need to find another. I suppose the bishop or Dad.*

The telephone rang.

Oh! Belle picked up the telephone receiver, "Hello, this is Belle."

"Belle," Caleb spoke. "I need to come by for some clothes and things. Are you going to be there for forty-five minutes? I can be finished by that time."

"Yes," she answered.

"Thank you. I'll be there in fifteen minutes."

It'll be my luck that Dr. Belknap will call when he's here. I'd like to talk to him but have to be able to talk to Dr. Belknap.

Although he technically still lived in the apartment, Caleb rang the doorbell when he arrived. As they discussed their situation, Caleb became angry, primarily with Church leaders for their unfulfilled promises. The telephone ring interrupted them.

"I need to take this. I'm expecting a call," Belle said.

Caleb walked into the bedroom to gather clothes he wanted.

"Hello," Belle said.

"Hi, this is Lou Belknap. Is this an okay time?"

"Thanks for calling. It's okay; Caleb is here to gather up a few things from the bedroom, but I said I was expecting an important call. Have you made an appointment for me?"

"Yes. Marla, or Ms. Hendricks I should say, is available a week from Friday afternoon from 3:00 on. That's the twenty-third. Does that still work for you?"

"Yes, that works fine. I can come to your office about 1:30 if that's okay for you."

"How about 12:15? Then we can go to this restaurant I've just heard of in Salt Lake City, have a bite of lunch, my treat. Then we go to see Ms. Hendricks, at least for now."

"That's good. You've made my day." Then Belle added. "Lou . . . ," and voice broke.

"What has happened?" Dr. Belknap asked.

"Well, when Caleb arrived, I started asking questions about us. He began explaining about his attraction to other men and the more he talked, the angrier he got. He walked into the bedroom when I answered the phone."

"Are you safe? Is he violent or threatening?"

"No, he hasn't threatened me, but he is angry. I don't think he would hit me or anything like that."

"Okay. If he does become threatening, get away; go outside. I'll be there. I'm home now, but I'm going to drive over to your place and park on the street near your apartment. I'll stay there until after he leaves. Anytime you feel threatened, come to my home or office for a refuge if you need to."

"Thanks. I think I'll be fine tonight."

"Please call me tomorrow or come by my office. I want to know how you're doing."

"Okay. Good night, and thanks for calling," Belle said.

Shortly after Belle hung up, Caleb came out of the bedroom with a box in which he had packed clothes. "I haven't got everything, just what I need for the time being. Later, I'll pack the rest, be out of your hair."

Caleb continued, "I'm staying with Tom Barker for the time being. The telephone number is written on this paper. I would like to remain friends with you, Belle. I am willing to talk over the issues with you as I see them. When I know more about where I'm staying on a more permanent basis, I'll call you to set a time when I can get the rest of my stuff."

And then, Caleb left.

He's being so arbitrary. I want to make this work, but he doesn't consider anything I say.

Belle was relieved to have spoken with Professor Belknap, to have an appointment, but her sense of peace did not remain. *What am I doing going to an inactive member of the Church? I should talk to mom and dad about this before taking my problems to others.*

Professor Belknap has helped so many women on campus.

Helped women? Or really lead them astray?

She's received praise from some of the administration. Surely that means she's okay. Oh, I don't know. Well, as I said before, if Ms. Hendricks requires a commitment up front that I. . . . Then it means I should not continue. Help me, Father. Inspire Ms. Hendricks to demand that commitment if this is wrong. Well, help me to know what I should do, independent of her position.

18
"Dr. Berniece Feltzer"

Belle did see Ms. Hendricks who, in the second visit, recommended that she make an appointment with Dr. Berniece Feltzer, the psychiatrist at the University Medical Center. For her first appointment with Dr. Feltzer, Belle drove to Salt Lake City, having borrowed the car—well, Caleb's car. She told him merely that she had to go for an appointment.

"Ms. Reynolds, please come to my office," said the woman who came through the hall and into the waiting room.

She looks intimidating, Belle thought. She noted the short brown hair which Dr. Feltzer combed over from a part on her right side to a single gold clip on the left. Above her temples, her hair was patched with gray. She walked with sturdy strides, confidently, firmly. *Her features,* Belle noted, *are rather usual, certainly not striking. Well, I can do this.*

"Come in," Dr. Feltzer instructed Belle. "Sit down."

"What brings you to see me?"

"I've been meeting with Ms. Marla Hendricks concerning my marriage—or the failure of my marriage. My husband says he's gay, homosexual, and…"

"Yes, I know what 'gay' means," Dr. Feltzer inserted. "I apologize for interrupting. Go on."

"Well, Ms. Hendricks has helped me see some things, and has tried to help me get beyond blaming myself so much. She says, however, that she doesn't know a lot of details, scientific studies, on homosexuality, so she recommended I come to you. I agreed."

294

"I see. Perhaps to start with, tell me about your courtship with, what's his name?"

"He's Caleb. We met, really met, when he got a teaching assistantship at BYU. I had previously been in the same class with him, but we didn't know each other; I don't think he even knew my name.

"Anyway, when he began as a TA, I was teaching for the second year. TAs have small carrels in two large rooms in the Maeser Building, and we had adjoining carrels for our offices. We got to know each other easily.

"We second-year TAs share ideas, visual aids, and other ideas with the new TAs just like the second-year TAs helped us when we were brand new to teaching. We spent a lot of time with each other both in the office and even out of the office as we had a class together. Shortly before Thanksgiving he asked me to a concert in the Fine Arts building. He also invited me to go Christmas caroling with his student ward."

"Did he kiss you goodnight after any of these occasions?"

"Oh, no. . . . Then in February, I think, he asked me to a party with the Intercollegiate Knights which he had joined as an undergraduate."

"When did he first kiss you? What was that date like?"

"Oh, I don't know for sure. I do remember wondering why he never tried to kiss me . . . thinking I could be unattractive to him, but he kept asking me out. I guess he kissed me first in the spring, maybe May or even June."

"Did he ever fondle your breasts?"

"Oh, that's right. . . I remember when he first kissed me. We were sitting in his car after we returned from a concert or play. I tucked a locket into my blouse as a safe place, while I played 'keep

296

away.' It may have been that I was mainly enticing him to get the locket, in other words, to get into light petting. That night at the door of my apartment, he kissed me."

"Tell me about the game of 'get my locket.'"

"Actually, it was a medallion, a small cameo, which my grandmother had owned. I don't remember how it began, but I did say, 'I'm not letting you get it' or something similar, and I slipped it under my blouse.

He rose to the challenge, saying 'Oh, yeah?' He stuck his hand down my blouse and grabbed the medallion; I grabbed the chain and tugged. The chain broke; he had the medallion but was immediately contrite. He apologized a lot for breaking the chain and handed back the medallion. He then got out of the car and opened my door for me. When we reached the apartment door, he kissed me once and left."

"How did you feel about the kiss?"

"I was a bit puzzled. He didn't seem very passionate. . . well, that's an understatement. He hadn't previously been very physical with me, tried anything. Actually, he only rarely held my hand . . . so the kiss was an improvement, but even that night, I realized he wasn't very passionate; it was like kissing one of my brothers."

"When he reached his hand into your blouse, did he fondle your breast?"

"No, I think he hardly even touched them."

"Did he ever get more physical with you in the remainder of your courtship?"

"Not really. He usually kissed me goodnight, but we didn't ever sit in a secluded spot and kiss or neck with each other. We did occasionally sit in the living room of my apartment and hold hands,

298

sometimes even cuddled, while watching
a TV program."

"When was your first sexual
contact?"

"Actually, we didn't even have
sex the night of our wedding. I didn't
connect that we didn't have sex with the
possibility that he might be gay. I just
focused on what did happen. When I
came out of the bathroom that night, he
was already in his pajamas, sitting on the
bed. He shook, shivered —uncontrollably.
I thought he was cold so we went to bed
and I held him in my arms. I guess it was
two or three nights later that we first had
sex."

"How did you feel about this?"

"I was a little disturbed. I
wondered if something was the matter
with me, if I had bad breath or
something."

"How did you proceed the second and third nights? You say that it was not until the third night that you had sex?"

"Well, the second night I brushed my teeth and rinsed my mouth out afterwards so I knew I didn't have bad breath. I brushed my hair well so it was soft and flowing and I didn't tie it up in any way. Still nothing.

"The third night I did the same preparation and then once in bed I approached him, put my arm around him. He rolled onto his side facing me and I kissed him and placed his hand on my breast. I rubbed his chest and focused on his nipples; he seemed to mimic my actions. I … I eventually moved my hand down to his genital area. Slowly, he became aroused."

"I sense that you are a bit uncomfortable talking to me about your sex life. But I think we should talk more about it. Do you talk with him about sex?"

300

"No, I haven't. Well, the next morning after the first time, I told him I had enjoyed the previous night."

"Well, we will talk more of this next time, if you wish to continue. Now our time is almost over. I have some suggested reading for you . . . if you wish to continue our sessions. Actually, I think these readings would be helpful to you regardless, but I would like you to read them especially if we continue."

"Yes, I think I should continue meeting with you."

"I have available a selection from a book known informally as the *Kinsey Study* written by Dr. Alfred Kinsey of the Kinsey Institute at Indiana University. Although the study has been out for well for over twenty years, I don't think BYU library has it. This excerpt comes from chapter 21 and concerns homosexuality.

"I also suggest a book by Alan Bell and Martin Weinberg entitled *Homosexualities: A Study of Diversity.*

This was published by Indiana University Press in 1978. Perhaps you can use your BYU student card to check it out from the Marriott Library at the 'U.' It might be at the library at BYU, but maybe not.

"When you come back, we can discuss the ideas on homosexuality—its causes, variability, and likelihood of being changed."

"How often should I plan to come?" Belle asked.

"If you can, come back in two weeks. Would that fit your schedule?"

"I think so. I'll call your office to verify."

On her drive back to Provo, Belle pondered the righteousness of this path. *What have I gotten into? Why am I seeking help from a non-member and not the bishop? And why is she having me read about homosexuality? I guess it's to help me understand Caleb and learn what I can do for him.*

302

*Can I find the book at the library?
Will BYU trace the book and know who
has checked it out. I don't want that. They
may even connect my reading it to Caleb
and put him on a watch list. Well, I can't
protect him all the time. I need to check
the book out.*

*Maybe I shouldn't be reading
these materials.*

*Stop! I already know I have to go
places intellectually, spiritually, where I
wouldn't go normally. I'm going to check
the book out . . . if BYU holds it.*

The next day, Saturday, Belle
went to the card catalog in the library to
search for the book Dr. Feltzer had
recommended and to see what other
books the library held which might help
her. She didn't find anything, so she was
particularly grateful Dr. Feltzer had
provided a copy of the Kinsey study.

Belle decided that Monday she
would call Dr. Feltzer's office to set an
appointment for Friday, two weeks after

her first appointment. She also asked the receptionist if the recommended readings were available in the library at the "U." She decided that she would go back a week before her appointment with Dr. Feltzer so she might use the library at the "U." Surprisingly, the University Library did not have much more.

"What did you learn about the causes of homosexuality from your reading?" Dr. Feltzer asked Belle in their appointment.

"I really don't know what the causes are. Some of the authors seem to say it is not an easy answer. Everyone who had a theory of the cause could document examples which did not fit as well as some examples which did."

"What cures did you find? And how successful did they appear to be?"

"I didn't read anywhere an account of a cure that the writer believed. I saw confusion, or at least no answer, as to the cause of homosexuality. Probably there are no simple answers to its cause even perhaps for any given individual. Most who talk about causes seem to arrive at no definite conclusion. Most writers I read seem to indicate that while there could be multiple causes, they suggest that choice doesn't seem to be one."

"What does this say about you and your husband?"

"I guess it means that Caleb was gay before he met me. He said as much to me when he asked me for a divorce. I tried to encourage him to let us work on our marriage, but he was emphatic that it wouldn't work. I was angry, and hurt, that he wouldn't even try."

"Has he ever talked about his efforts to change? I'm assuming he did try as a faithful Latter-Day Saint."

"I remember his talking about that, but I don't remember any details. I guess I was too busy trying to get him to see my point of view."

305

"Then you think he did make an effort before you married to change his orientation?"

"He said so. He got quite angry when I didn't accept his words, so I'm quite sure he did. It's not like him to lie."

"This understanding bears directly upon your situation. Most importantly, if Caleb's homosexuality is not a choice, if it is more innate to him, then what is your responsibility in Caleb's coming out as gay?"

"I hadn't even thought of that! Now I see that Ms. Hendricks had been trying to help me see that, but she didn't approach the issue from the causation of homosexuality, but from the point of view of encouraging me to realize my own qualities."

"There are people, however, who believe that homosexuality is a choice and can be cured. I imagine you can find a book or two by Mr. Socarides, a writer who lives in California, in the BYU

306

library. There is also a PhD thesis at BYU which is available here at the University but may not be available at BYU because of the nature of the study. This latter work discusses electro-shock therapy to try to convert homosexuals to heterosexuality. You may find it quite unpleasant reading.

I will add that I have heard both directly and indirectly of the brutality of these conversion attempts. Moreover, most homosexuals who participated in these experiments have reported long-lasting negative effects. None whom I have talked to personally have become heterosexual.

"For our next meeting, I suggest we continue discussing the issue of homosexuality if you have questions on that topic. If you read the PhD thesis at BYU, you may have things you'd like to discuss.

Additionally, I'd like you to also work on your thoughts about the role of sex—actually, the role of romance and companionship—in a woman's life. What do you want in a relationship? See what books are available in the library at BYU on women. How do you respond to these books? What do they have to say that resonates with you?"

With those comments, they set up another appointment for two weeks. As she drove back to Provo, Belle thought about their conversation. *I appreciate Dr. Feltzer's helping me see that I'm not responsible for Caleb's being gay. I'm free! What a relief! I want to see Caleb and make amends for not understanding his. . . his desperation. I hope we can remain friends.*

I don't know how we get divorced so he doesn't get in trouble with the university. Even some of the faculty who know him may not be understanding. We must be careful.

I'm so excited with my freedom that I haven't even thought about Dr. Feltzer's instructions to think about what I want in a relationship. Oh, golly. What do I want? I thought Caleb was what I wanted. Now I want to be his friend and spend time with him and others doing whatever. But what do I want in a husband? I suppose that's what Dr. Feltzer wants me to explore: what I want in a sexual, friendly relationship, not just close friends.

It's possible we'll have to keep our situation hidden until graduation. Wow. That'll be hard. Yes, hard on me, but really hard on Caleb. Maybe we should continue living together, but I don't know if he will trust me that much. We need to talk.

19
"Further Light and Knowledge"

On Saturday, the day after her visit with Dr. Feltzer, Belle returned to BYU Library to search for books on homosexuality, especially the PhD dissertation Dr. Feltzer had mentioned. In the subject card catalog, she tried "gays," "gay Mormons," "homosexuality," all without success. Finally, she tried "Theses," "Dissertations," which brought up numerous hits. *I can't go through all these cards searching for one thesis, truly a needle in a haystack.* She gave up and went to work on her own homework.

On Monday a week after her second visit to Dr. Feltzer, Belle dropped into Dr. Belknap's office near the end of her office hours.

"Belle! How good to see you," Lou Belknap greeted her at the door of her office. "Come in and sit down. Tell me what's going on in your life."

"Lou, it has been such an amazing three or four weeks. I saw Ms. Hendricks a couple of times, and she recommended I see Dr. Feltzer at the University of Utah Medical Center. I've seen her a couple of times, and she has really helped me. From the beginning Dr. Feltzer had me reading about homosexuality. The books she had me read discussed the causes—none of these writers could identify definite causes—and then I realized it is not choice and it is not curable; I cannot blame myself for Caleb's being gay. What a relief that was!

"What I've noticed is that the library here has only a very little about homosexuality, and what they have is quite anti-homosexual. They don't agree on the cause, but they all condemn homosexuals as selfish, perverted, dirty-old-men-type predators. Caleb isn't any of those things. I could see the writers are definitely wrong about that. I also read the chapter on homosexuality in the original Kinsey study; Dr. Feltzer had that copied for me. That study doesn't seek for a cause or cast blame on anyone. They show that homosexuals are people, humans with sexual preferences that simply differ from those of heterosexuals. Perfectly normal."

"Are you still meeting with Marla Hendricks?"

"I have an arrangement I can call her to set up an appointment whenever I feel a need to get back to her, but I haven't gone for two or three weeks now."

"Are you still going to see Dr. Feltzer?"

"Yes. My most recent assignment has been to decide what I want in a husband. Dr. Feltzer left that term out; she said 'in a relationship.' I suppose she is allowing me to decide to have a man without marriage."

"I'm sure she said it that way so as to leave you in charge of that decision."

"I know. It's so exciting to be the one who chooses. To feel she accepts whatever I decide. It's so thrilling, yet scary, to be so free."

"Well, I think that you must be as hungry as I am. Let's get supper, then I'll take you home."

"Well, I have so much to do for my classes; I've neglected them horribly over the past two months."

"You need to eat. An hour or so off won't hurt your schedule and going out with me will spare you the cooking and cleanup."

"You're right. I'm all yours."

Near the end of their fourth session, Dr. Feltzer asked, "Belle, have you ever looked at or touched your genitalia?"

"No," Belle stammered. "Why? That isn't something I would do, even consider doing."

"Did you not play 'doctor' as a child?"

"Well, yes. A couple of times with a neighbor boy."

"But you were never the doctor?"

"No."

"I suggest you take a mirror, and in a well-lighted place, you examine yourself. Discover that aspect of yourself."

On her drive back to Provo, Belle pondered Dr. Feltzer's suggestion. *Why had I never been 'doctor.' I guess I really didn't want to be 'doctor.' I don't remember even having a class in high school about sex. I never saw my brothers or dad naked. I never even saw mom naked.*

Boys always seemed to initiate playing 'doctor.' Girls were always the patients, never the doctor. Do little girls get to be the doctor now? Surely the old

314

*argument that girls are not doctors no
longer holds true.*

*Maybe it is time I became a
'doctor.'*

That's revolutionary.

*Would it be proper? Maybe not,
but. . .*

After she returned to her
apartment, she stalled, finding this job
and that duty that needed doing. Finally,
after eating supper and cleaning up the
dishes afterwards, she went toward the
bedroom. She stopped at the bathroom
door.

*Maybe I should do this here with
the door closed so no one. . . Oh, come
on, no one lives with me. Who could see
me? I'll be more comfortable on the bed.*

She went into the bathroom,
retrieved her hand mirror, and walked to
the bedroom.

315

She laid the hand mirror on her bed and walked to the closet as she removed her blouse. She hung up her blouse, then took off her skirt, hanging it in the closet. She glanced at the window to verify the curtains were closed, then went to the dresser to retrieve her nightgown. Instead of putting it on, she laid it on the double bed she and Caleb had shared.

How do I do this? Well, if I'm going to do it, I may as well do it right.

She removed her arms from the temple garment, lowered it and stepped out of the garment, then laid it carefully on the bed beside her nightgown. She shivered.

That first night, Caleb shivered, uncontrollably. Am I doing something wrong? Something I'll regret?

Okay, let's do this.

She arranged pillows at the head of the bed, sat down on it and leaned against the pillows. She picked up the hand mirror, spread her legs apart, and positioned the mirror between them. She looked.

Ah. "A well-lighted place," Dr. Feltzer said.

She quickly glanced around the room and decided the bed was still the best place for this. She switched ends of the bed, placing the pillows at the foot of the bed so she would be comfortably propped up and able to see. She lay down. The lamps on the bedside tables now dispelled the shadows; she picked up the mirror and spread her legs.

"Oh!" she exclaimed. She extended her free hand and touched, then stroked again, then again. She soared below the physical, plunged high beyond metaphor.

Oh, Mother of all living! she thought. *Creator of all. O Mystery. Ah. Through Thy grace do we exist.*

In the days afterwards, she saw the authors in literature differently, questioning each individually, pondering their writings. *Hemingway never saw beyond his own penis. Lawrence, maybe. In* Sons and Lovers, *he doesn't seem to have. . . but the gardener in* Lady Chatterley's Lover *may have truly known.*

I'm sure Dickinson knew. How different her poetry may become as I reread! I think George Elliot saw; Dorothea grows into this independence, this understanding.

Did Jane Austen know? Why would she portray Elizabeth not gaining this awareness if she herself had it?

Maybe she would not have allowed herself to stray into such a socially inappropriate place. This could be the ultimate example of Austen's "not dropping a stitch." Yes, perhaps Austen knew, but governed her awareness to meet the requirements of her novel, actually, of her audience. I like that idea.

20
"Another Reunion"

On a July visit to Draper, CT asked Caleb how Belle was doing. Caleb said he visited with her two days previous. "She's finished her thesis and defends it on Friday. I'm sure she'll do well. I'm meeting her immediately afterwards and we'll go out to eat and a movie to celebrate."

Emma asked, "Will you bring her up for a visit? I'd like to see her. We could prepare a celebration supper. Would that work out for you?" she asked Caleb. "Could we do it, say, Sunday afternoon?"

"Yes, I think so. I'm quite sure she'd like to come visit with you as well," Caleb answered. "I'll check to see if that day is open for her."

Caleb and Belle went to visit his parents on the last Sunday in July. Belle had looked forward to this visit since

Caleb had told her his parents would like to continue having her in their lives, if she was okay with that. "They'd like to do a celebration lunch in honor of your finishing the thesis and passing your oral exams."

It was not until they were already driving to Draper from Provo that Belle began thinking more deeply about the visit. Questions arose in her mind.

Are either Emma or CT going to ask me to stop divorce proceedings? Am I going to feel forced to take sides in a disagreement? I don't want to take sides. I don't want this to be Caleb versus his parents. Or even Caleb against either of his parents. Oh, dear.

She turned to Caleb. "How are your parents taking your being gay?"

"Dad seems to be okay. He's told me he thinks we are making a mistake to divorce, or even separate. Mom wants me to save the marriage, to make it work."

"Well, you obviously feel relatively comfortable with them, in spite of their disagreeing with you, with us."

"Yes, dad's told me that though he disapproves, he supports me. He said I'm always welcome in his home, regardless."

"That's got to be a comfort to you."

"Yes, it is. I don't know how he'll take my looking for a companion or even dating. But that will have to wait until I transfer from the 'Y.'"

"Have you sent applications to other universities?"

"Yes, to the 'U,' to Cal Berkeley, and to Arizona. But it's so late in the application period I doubt I'll even be considered."

They sat silent as they left the freeway and began driving through the streets toward the home where Emma and CT lived. Belle again thought about the awkwardness of her position. Then she reflected on her own struggle with Caleb's coming out.

I didn't agree with Caleb when he first told me. But I've come to understand so much more over time. And I know Emma and CT won't want to make me feel awkward; they won't put me in a tough spot. I'll relate my experiences with Dr. Belknap and to an extent with Dr. Feltzer.

They drove into the driveway, climbed out of the car and walked to the door into the kitchen.

"Hi, anybody home?" Caleb called out as he entered the kitchen.

"Come in, come in," called Emma as she walked from the living room, where she and CT had been reading, through the dining room and toward the kitchen. "It's so good to see you. O, Belle, thanks for coming. We've missed you."

CT followed Emma into the kitchen. Emma hugged Belle, then Caleb. CT shook hands with Caleb and placed his left hand on Caleb's shoulder, squeezed it, and then gave Belle a hug.

"If you came directly from church, you're probably starved. I've got the makings for a picnic-type lunch that we can eat in the cool of the kitchen rather than outside in the heat. The table's all set; you each choose wherever you'd like to sit. I'll pull things out of the fridge. CT, please get the sodas and fruit juices from the fridge."

Emma pulled a roasted ham from the fridge and began to cut slices from it to place on a platter, and then she retrieved a small platter, covered with lines of fresh carrots and shelled peas from her garden. Finally, she pulled out a large bowl with a lettuce, tomato, and cucumber salad.

Caleb retrieved bottles of mustard and the blue cheese and French dressings for the salad. CT put ice cubes in four glasses and filled a pitcher with more ice cubes and water. He also grabbed some sodas from the fridge for anyone who might want something besides water. The preparations stopped conversation.

CT said the blessing on the food. "Our Father in Heaven, we are thankful Belle and Caleb have joined us today. Our time together today is a celebration to congratulate Belle on finishing her master's degree. We ask Thee to bless the food for our nourishment and health. In the name of Jesus Christ, Amen."

Then, after everyone said "Amen," they served themselves from the dishes.

"What are your plans now you've finished?" CT asked Belle.

"I'll be teaching freshman composition full-time at the 'Y.' They've offered me a temporary position; I'm sure that to move into a permanent position, I'll have to do a PhD somewhere, of course, but I haven't planned that far

324

ahead. The 'Y' doesn't offer a PhD in English."

"How has your degree progressed?" CT asked Caleb.

"I need another semester. I've taken enough courses but will have to take a class while I finish writing my thesis. I expect to finish by December, in plenty of time for May graduation next year," Caleb admitted. "As you know, I had considered transferring to the 'U' or some other university, but as I haven't heard from any of them, I'm quite sure I'll have to finish at the 'Y.'"

"Why will that be bad?" CT asked.

"Well, as I think I told you earlier, now that I've said I'm gay, some in the University administration would want me expelled, even though I haven't done anything," Caleb said.

"Are there specific administrators who have said you particularly should be expelled?" CT asked.

"No," Caleb answered. "Only that they have said that anyone who talks about being homosexual is promoting it and therefore breaking the Honor Code. So, for those administrators, I've already done enough to warrant their expelling me."

"This situation makes Caleb's position so tenuous," Belle inserted. "The way some administrators at the 'Y' work, they could decide to expel him anytime even though he just needs a semester to finish and defend his thesis.

"I appreciate your invitation," Belle said. "I have really enjoyed being part of your lives, and this...."

Emma filled the silence following Belle's pause. "We love you and hope we can continue seeing you."

326

"I hope you can understand, even if you disagree with our decision to separate and eventually divorce, Caleb and I have come to an agreement. I wasn't there at first; I didn't agree for quite some time, but I now think he's right. We continue as good friends."

"You're okay with this separation?" Emma asked.

"I know it will be hard on both of us, especially as we're both in the same department at the 'Y.' We have to be careful to avoid saying we are separating.

"I guess I'm most aware of my future difficulties. Divorced women in the Church have a difficult life ahead of them. There are bound to be people in any ward where I live who will see me as a pariah, as a threat to their marriages, or in the case of single men as a castoff. But eventually, I can marry again and be acceptable in the Church."

"And you, Caleb," CT asked. "Are you planning to remain active in the Church?"

"Right now, the Church seems awkward and unpleasant for me. I don't know what will happen. I can't say and certainly won't make any firm commitments about the future."

"Surely you aren't going to start living a gay lifestyle," Emma demanded.

"I honestly don't know what's going to happen. I don't know . . . I don't want to live alone. I. . ." He paused, breathed. "I want a companion, a man whom I can love and be loved by. I realize that will probably cost me my Church membership."

"Oh, you make my heart ache," Emma said.

"As I said earlier, Caleb, you are our son and you're welcome in our home. We disagree with you, but we love you, dearly," CT said.

328

"Yes, we do," Emma said quickly. "And we will pray for you always."

The conversation turned to less intense topics, the weather, the major league baseball season, plans for upcoming holidays. Belle especially enjoyed talking about plans for the break between summer school and fall semester, now her degree work was done.

The conversation did not turn to Belle's becoming reconciled to Caleb's position. The opportunity to relate any of her experiences with Dr. Belknap, Ms. Hendricks, or Dr. Feltzer didn't occur.

21
"Liberating Emma"

By this stage of her life, Emma was really alone. Aunt Mary had passed away while still only middle aged, and Emma had no other confidant. So she buried her doubts and her feelings of inadequacies deep in her heart, pondering them only when they thrust themselves upon her. She gradually began contrasting her horror of Caleb's confession to CT's reaction. CT was saddened by Caleb's decision, but he didn't mourn; that confused her.

Does he not know this is Caleb's damnation? Does he not care for Caleb's eternal welfare? Was his lack of real involvement in Caleb's youth a cause of Caleb's becoming gay? Isn't that what the prophets have taught: a distant father and a smothering, dominant mother? Oh, then, I, too, must be guilty. Oh, my God. Father, what have I done?

330

For months after Caleb told her he and Belle were divorcing and why, she mourned, holding her self-condemnation inside. She remained stoic in public; her mourning was solitary. While she tried to remain dispassionate whenever Caleb came home, she noted that CT was totally relaxed, at ease with Caleb. He didn't seem at all aloof; they talked and laughed.

What's wrong with them? Why doesn't CT chastise Caleb, tell him what is right, explain the truth? One Sunday afternoon while Caleb and CT were talking as usual, Emma thought, *Is CT homosexual also? Is that why he's so comfortable with this? What does this mean for our celestial marriage? Will I be alone hereafter?* That night her prayers included her worries about CT. *If he is homosexual also, was he spending those nights so many years ago in Salt Lake City with men?*

One night she knelt as usual in private prayer beside her bed. This night, however, was quietly different. As she once again poured out her sorrow to the

Lord, she felt peace come over her. Divine love engulfed her. She realized God held her blameless in Caleb's and CT's lives. She knew God loved her. And God loved them. Peace filled her, flowed through her, buoyed her up.

[This page left intentionally blank]

[This page left intentionally blank]

MORMON VOCABULARY

c. James F. Cartwright, 2015,
revised and enlarged 2020, 2022.

*I learned from comments/questions
from participants in Writers' Workshop at
Lutheran Church of Honolulu, that Mormons
often use vocabulary non-Mormons do not
understand. A portion of the confusion arises
from the unique polity of the Mormon
Church: some terms used in common with
other Christian denominations do not carry
the same meaning in Mormon polity; other
terms are unique to Mormonism. In addition,
some terms explained here have local
meaning. I first used the "Mormon
Vocabulary" in an earlier publication,*
Symphonia. *In this version, I have used bold
type for main entries and for terms which are
defined elsewhere in the vocabulary.*

"AC, the": Utah colloquialism for Utah
State Agriculture College. Since 1957,
Utah State University.

Bishop: The bishop in the Mormon
Church is the local leader of a **Ward** or
congregation made up of approximately

300 to 600 members. His position and authority compare with the parish pastor in a typical Christian congregation. His tenure is usually for three years, after which he is released and frequently given another calling. He selects two counselors from male ward members; together they form the bishopric of the ward.

Celestial Room: This is the final place in the temple endowment ceremony. It represents the place where God lives and thus is the goal for mortals. The **Veil** of the temple separates the preceding stages of the endowment from the Celestial Room.

Councils of Seventy: For many years there was only one Council of Seventy, composed of seventy men who assisted the members of the **Quorum of Twelve Apostles** in conducting church affairs throughout the world. These men were also **High Priests** and held lifetime appointments. As the work of the church expanded with growing membership, additional councils of seventy were organized. Members of these additional

336

councils of seventy are not called for their lifetime, but are released after a period of time.

Courts: a court is a disciplinary action undertaken by the Church to punish a form of disobedience. Courts may be held by the bishop and his counselors if the person being disciplined is a woman or a man who does not hold the **Melchizedek Priesthood.** Men who hold the Melchizedek Priesthood must be tried by the **stake high council** and **stake presidency**.

Deseret (dĕzêrĕt´): The word comes from the *Book of Mormon* meaning *honey bee*. The word became popular in Mormon areas. The proposed State of Deseret was a Mormon application to the United States Congress for statehood, proposed in 1850. Some towns have been named Deseret, as have institutions such as Deseret Gym, Deseret Bank, and the University of Deseret, the initial name of the University of Utah.

Elder: An office within the Melchizedek Priesthood. Men called as missionaries are now ordained Elders, thus most Elders are quite young in age, beginning at age eighteen.

Endowment: A ceremony conducted in a Mormon Temple in which individuals receive blessings and make promises concerning their lives. The endowment ceremony is a symbolic tracing of life: persons symbolically follow the path of Adam and Eve through creation to the Garden of Eden to the Fall and then to a paradisaical state followed by an entrance to God's presence in the Celestial Kingdom. Because the ceremony is viewed as a necessary step in one's progress to return to the presence of God, Mormons also perform the endowment for those who have died without the opportunity of doing this while living. Faithful Mormons who have already taken out their own endowment return to the temple as proxies for someone who has died. One usually takes out their own endowment before going on a mission or getting married.

First Presidency: The **President of the Church** and his councilors make up the First Presidency. The president is also called the Prophet, Seer, and Revelator for the Church and the world. He becomes the president by becoming the senior member in years of service within the **Quorum of Twelve Apostles**.

Garments: See **Temple Garment(s)**

General Authorities: A generic term referring to the First Presidency, the Quorum of the Twelve Apostles, and the (First) Council of Seventy.

High Priests: An office in the **Melchizedek Priesthood**. All members of ward bishoprics, stake presidencies and high councils, and the general authorities of the church are high priests.

Lay Priesthood: All Mormon officials are lay ministers in that they have no academic or professional training for their appointment. Only the men in the Quorum of Twelve Apostles, the First Council of Seventy, and the First

Presidency have life-time calls. All other officers have temporary calls: bishops usually for three years, stake presidents for five years, and members of other Councils of Seventy for three to five years.

Melchizedek Priesthood is the higher priesthood in the Mormon Church with the Aaronic Priesthood, the lesser priesthood, being for boys ages 12 to 18. The Melchizedek Priesthood has three offices, **High Priest**, **Seventy**, and **Elder**. Men are ordained Elders when they leave for missionary work, now often at age 18; by the time they are in their late twenties, they are now ordained high priests; the office of seventy is now limited to the **Councils of the Seventy.**

Priesthood: Only men are ordained to the priesthood. Before 1978 but after the death of the Prophet Joseph Smith, men of African descent were prohibited from being ordained; the Prophet Joseph ordained some African Americans to the priesthood. During the nineteenth century and perhaps early twentieth century, some groups of Pacific Islanders may also have been prohibited from the Melchizedek Priesthood.

Quorum of Twelve Apostles: After the First Presidency, the Quorum of Twelve Apostles is the highest governing body of the Mormon Church. It consists of twelve high priests chosen by other members of the Quorum and the First Presidency to fill vacancies within the Quorum when a death reduces the number in the First Presidency or the Quorum.

RM: Colloquialism for returned missionary.

Sealing: The portion of the temple ceremony which unites couples with their spouses and children to their parents for eternity. Sealings are done for the living and vicariously for those who have died.

Stake: This organizational level within the Mormon Church is similar to a diocese or synod in some Christian churches. A stake consists of a group of local **Wards** or congregations in the

Mormon Church. The stake is presided over by a President and his councilors (usually two), comprising the stake presidency.

Stake High Council: An advisory body made up of twelve men from within the stake. All the men in the stake presidency and high council are **High Priests**. Members of the stake presidency and the stake high council are frequently released after three to five years. Members of the high council are called by the stake president with approval of his councilors and high council.

Temple: A Mormon temple is a separated, holy place with a specific worship within. It is only available to faithful members of the church who must obtain a recommend through an interview process, including separate interviews with the ward bishop and then with the stake president. As the member passes each interview, the authority adds his signature to the recommend. The recommend is valid for one year only, after which a new one is issued through the same interview process. One is not allowed to enter the temple itself without a valid, current, recommend.

Temple Garment(s): Part of the endowment includes being clothed in a sacred undergarment. The individual is expected to wear a corollary garment, slightly different from the garment used in the temple, at all times. The garment is frequently referred to in the plural form, **Garments.**

Temple Worker: A man or woman who has accepted the calling to work in the temple, helping people who have come to the temple either for their own endowment or as proxy for someone who has died. The men called as temple workers hold the Melchizedek Priesthood.

Tracting: The practice of Mormon missionaries going through a neighborhood, knocking on the door of every house to ask if the occupants would be willing to hear a message about the Mormon Church. The term may have originated from the tract of land on which a residential area was built or, more likely, from the religious pamphlets or tracts the missionaries give to anyone willing to accept one.

Trunky: Missionary idiom describing a missionary anxious to be released to return home; from "sitting on his suitcase or trunk."

"U, the": Colloquialism for the University of Utah.

Veil: The veil refers to that which separates mortals from God. Specifically in the temple ritual, it is the place at the end of the endowment where the person who is attending the temple either for themself or for a person who has died, is "tested" on the covenants made during the ceremony before being admitted through the veil into the presence of God. **Temple workers** accompany people attending the temple to the veil where they prompt the people if they need help answering the questions. A worker in the temple plays the role of the divine being asking the questions at the veil.

Ward: A local congregation in Mormonism. With exception of some particular cases, wards are geographical in nature, similar to a parish in traditional Christianity. In the Mormon Church, however, a member's opting to attend and belong to a neighboring ward is rarely allowed; one belongs to the ward in which she or he lives.

Washing and Anointing: First part of the temple ceremony for the living. When work is done for the dead, baptism is the first step in the temple ceremony; baptism for living persons is performed at least one year prior to their going to the Temple. The baptism and washing and anointing portions for the deceased person are frequently separated from the endowment and sealing portions. As a result, people attending the temple usually only perform the endowment portion.

"Y, the": Colloquialism for Brigham Young University.

"Mormon Vocabulary," copyright, 2015, revised, 2020.

About the Author

James Farmer Cartwright grew up in Draper, Utah, in the southeast corner of Salt Lake Valley. He attended Brigham Young University for two years before serving as a missionary in the West Spanish American Mission of the L.D.S. Church from October 1961 to April 1964. He returned to BYU, earning a bachelor's degree in 1966 and a master's degree in English in 1969. Later, he completed a master's degree in history at the University of Utah and a master's degree in Library Science at the University of California, Berkeley.

He taught English composition at BYU and Weber State College and English literature and composition with the University of Maryland, European Division. He worked seven years as archives assistant at Weber State before going to the University of California, Berkeley. After completing his MLS at Cal, he became University Archivist at

346

the University of Hawai'i, retiring after twenty-five years in 2013.

He has written various short stories over thirty plus years, of which he has published five in two volumes available on Amazon.com. One short story, "Brothers," is an e-book; *Symphonia,* containing four stories, is available in print.

For the past twenty-eight years, he has participated in the Lutheran Church of Honolulu. After officially joining LCH, he served two terms on the congregational council. Years later, in December 2021, he was elected to another term on the council. He sang in the choir of LCH for about twenty years. He has participated in the Audit, the Music and Worship, and the Pastoral Intern Support committees.

In September 1996, he met his life partner, Wally Mahan; they married 26 August 2008 in San Francisco. In December 2015, he resigned his membership in the Mormon Church.

[This page left intentionally blank.]